FOOTBALL CHAMP

HarperCollins*Publishers*

TBALL
AMP

TIM GREEN

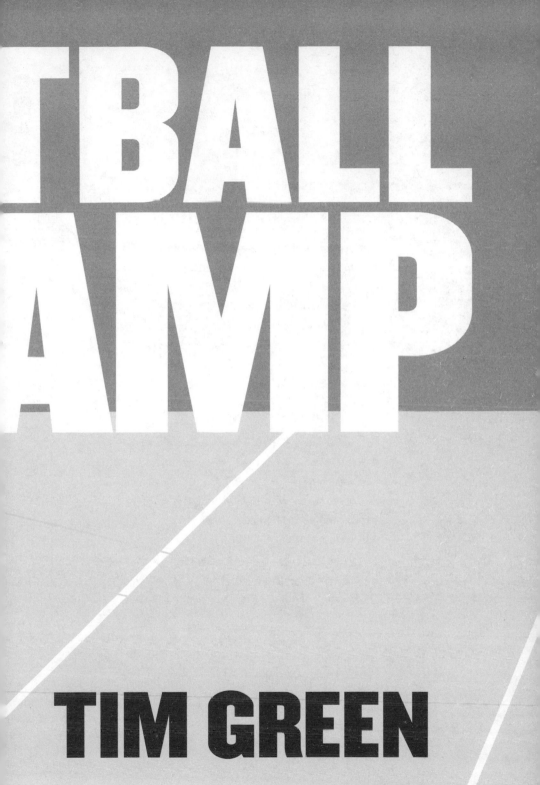

Football Champ

 For information address HarperCollins Children's Books, a division of HarperCollins Publishers, 10 East 53rd Street, New York, NY 10022.

www.harpercollinschildrens.com

Library of Congress Cataloging-in-Publication Data

Green, Tim, date

Football champ / Tim Green. — 1st ed.

p. cm.

Summary: Twelve-year-old Troy's uncanny gift for predicting football plays proves a powerful secret weapon for the Atlanta Falcons, but a seedy reporter with a vendetta suspects something is going on and sets out to shred the reputations of Troy and star linebacker Seth Halloway.

ISBN 978-0-06-162689-0 (trade bdg.)

ISBN 978-0-06-162690-6 (lib. bdg.)

[1. Football—Fiction. 2. Reporters and reporting—Fiction. 3. Secrets—Fiction. 4. Atlanta Falcons (Football team)—Fiction. 5. Atlanta (Ga.)—Fiction.] I. Title.

PZ7.G826357Fok 2009 2008051775

[Fic]—dc22 CIP

AC

Typography by Joel Tippie

09 10 11 12 13 LP/RRDH 10 9 8 7 6 5 4 3 2 1

❖

First Edition

For my kids, Thane, Tessa, Troy, Tate, and Ty,
and their champ of a mom, Ilyssa

CHAPTER ONE

TROY KNEW BETTER THAN to push the NFL coach aside and signal the play himself for everyone to see. Troy was a secret. The Falcons were winning, 17–13, but the Bears had the ball on the Falcons' five-yard line, and there was time for one last play. If the Falcons' defense held, the game would be over and the team's run at the playoffs would be real.

"You're sure?" the coach asked, pain in his eyes as the smoke from his breath drifted skyward in the cold Chicago air.

The Bears' offense broke the huddle and started for the line. Seth Halloway, the Falcons' star linebacker, waved his hands to Troy and the coach, frantic for a defensive play.

"Yes," Troy said impatiently. "They're going to run the slant."

He knew adults doubted twelve-year-olds, anyway. His calls had been good enough in the last three games for the Falcons to end a losing streak and beat the Raiders, Tampa Bay, and New Orleans. Troy stared hard into the defensive coordinator's eyes until the older man blinked, turned, and signaled in Troy's play.

Seth nodded at the signal and shouted the play to his defensive teammates, cupping his hands over his mouth. The center snapped the ball. The defense blitzed. The quarterback dropped and threw the slant.

Seth Halloway leaped in front of the receiver and snatched the ball, securing the Falcons' fourth win in a row.

Troy jumped almost as high as Seth. So did every other player and coach on the Falcons' sideline. The defensive coach hugged Troy. Players smacked his back and hooted with joy. Some of them called out his name, and Troy's face burned with pride.

They knew him and they knew what he did.

Even though officially he was a ball boy, the players *knew.*

Troy saw Seth in the mayhem and grinned, but Seth didn't grin back.

"Come quick," Seth said, leading Troy by the arm and pushing through the crowd of NFL players and into the dark tunnel.

"Why?" Troy asked, searching Seth's face. "Let's celebrate!"

"That reporter, Peele, he saw you. We've got to get you out of here before he ruins everything."

CHAPTER TWO

"I'M A BALL BOY," Troy said, reciting the line he'd been given by the team owner and coaches.

"He saw the defensive coordinator of an NFL team talking to a kid in a parka and a hat before every call was made," Seth said, limping and looking over his shoulder. "But Peele doesn't know *who* you are and he doesn't know your mom works for the team, and we need to keep it that way."

Troy's mom appeared in the sea of shoulder pads, torn tape, grass-stained jerseys, and bloody knuckles. Her fingers clutched a clipboard tight enough to make them white. She threw a worried look at Troy. As part of the team's public relations staff, she worked with the media all the time. If she thought the man after

Troy now would hurt them all if he could, Troy knew it to be true.

"That way," she said, pointing down the opposite tunnel from where the players streamed, cheering and chanting on their way to the locker-room victory celebration. "Hurry. I'll slow him down. Kenny Albert's going to help us. Don't worry, Troy. I'll meet you at the airport, at the Delta desk."

"Kenny Albert the TV announcer?" Troy asked. "I'm not going to the airport with the team?"

"You can't ride the bus. We've got to keep a lid on this thing," Seth said, swinging open a metal door with a bang and leading Troy through a room where red and blue cables lay snaked across the floor.

"But we're not doing anything wrong," Troy said.

"Sometimes that doesn't matter," Seth said, leading Troy out into an enormous garage where four huge tractor-trailers sprouting more cables stood in a row. "Sometimes if it *looks* wrong, it's just as bad, especially with a newspaper reporter. Especially with Peele."

As Troy and Seth dodged between the television trucks and their colorful spray of cables, several technicians patted Seth on the shoulder and said what a great game he played. Seth thanked them but never stopped moving toward the exit. Opening the metal door, he peered quickly out into the cold dusk, looking both ways before he grabbed Troy and hauled him out to a waiting black Town Car. In front of the limo, a police car sat with the blue lights spinning silently atop its roof.

"What's the cop car for?" Troy asked.

"Police escort to the airport," Seth said. "For Kenny."

Two men stood beside the Town Car, both hunched over against the cold Chicago twilight with their hands stuffed into the pockets of their dark overcoats. Troy recognized the dark-haired man from television.

"That's Kenny Albert," Troy said in a whisper to Seth.

"Yeah, he's a friend."

"Did he ever interview you?" Troy asked.

"Sure."

"Hey, Seth," Kenny said, stepping forward. "Great game. We had you for seventeen tackles, two sacks, and an interception. Looks like a run at the playoffs."

The announcer signaled the other man, who climbed in and revved the engine.

"You okay with taking Troy?" Seth asked. "Brent Peele is looking for him. Things could get ugly."

Kenny smiled at Troy, patting his shoulder, and said, "No problem. I told Tessa I'd help. She's his mom, right? She's great, and I owe you for giving me the inside scoop on that thing with Coach Krock. Whose business is it who rides in my car, anyway?"

"Uh," Seth said, looking over his shoulder, "Kenny, just keep him down low. Tessa doesn't want Peele to know he's her son or to get a picture of him for the paper or something. All Peele could see from the press box was a kid on the sideline talking to the coaches."

"Hey, whatever you guys want is good," Kenny said. "Here, I'll get my garment bag, and if we need to I can even cover him up."

Kenny popped open the deep trunk and hauled out his garment bag.

The sound of men shouting rose up from behind them. Seth spun and stepped in front of Troy, hiding him.

"Seth!" someone shouted. "Hey, Halloway! Seth Halloway!"

"It's Peele," Seth said in a hiss.

Troy looked around in sudden panic. He heard Peele approaching. There was just one place to go where the reporter wouldn't see him. He dove into the trunk and curled up, signaling Kenny to close it. Kenny gave him a look of surprise, and Troy signaled the announcer to hurry. He watched Kenny's hand grip the trunk's edge and slam it shut.

The complete and sudden darkness sent a fresh surge of panic through Troy's body, but a cry from outside the car, right next to Seth now, kept him from making a sound.

"Seth!" Peele shouted. "Hey! Halloway!"

"What?" Seth asked, his voice stiff and cold.

"So, what's going on?" Peele said, breathless, but loud enough to hear through the trunk. "What are you doing here? Where's that kid I saw you talking to on the sideline?"

"What kid?" Seth said.

Silence followed before Peele said, "I'm not stupid. You're running around the last four games like you know the other team's plays, and then I notice some kid on the sideline in the coach's ear and then you whisk him away. Who is he?"

"I don't know what you're talking about," Seth said. "I got a plane to catch."

"Sure," Peele said. "So, what's in the trunk?"

CHAPTER THREE

TROY FELT THE RUMBLE of the big car's engine and caught a whiff of exhaust.

"None of your business," Seth said.

"You don't think so?" Peele asked.

"I got a plane to catch, too," Kenny Albert said. "Good luck next week, Seth."

"You in on this?" Peele asked.

"I have no idea what you're talking about," Kenny said. "Write that."

Troy heard the door shut.

An angry fist banged on the trunk as the car began to roll away.

"Maybe I will," Peele shouted. "Maybe that's just what I'll write."

The car picked up speed, made a couple of turns, and

slowed. Then it swerved and sped faster, with the police siren wailing ahead of it.

When they finally came to a stop and the trunk sprang open, Troy heard the roar of planes taking off. He climbed out and wrinkled his nose at the smell of jet fuel. The cop car drove away, and Kenny popped out of the limo with his garment bag.

"That Peele's kind of a jerk," Kenny said, "trying to hassle you just because of Seth."

"Seth?" Troy said, stretching his legs.

"He never told you?" Kenny asked.

Troy shook his head.

"I have to run to catch my plane," Kenny said, "but walk with me and I'll tell you."

"I'm meeting my mom at the Delta desk," Troy said.

"It's right near where I'm going," Kenny said. "Come on."

Troy walked alongside the announcer.

"My producer knew Peele from college," Kenny said. "Peele was actually a player, or he tried to be."

"Where?" Troy asked.

"Marist."

"That's where Seth played."

"I know," Kenny said, passing through the airport doors. "Seth had a scholarship, but Peele walked on to try to make the team as a receiver. One day in training camp, Peele came across the middle on a crossing pattern. It was a clean hit, but Seth basically ended his career."

"His career?" Troy said, hustling alongside the announcer.

"Not that he really had one," Kenny said, showing the woman at the security line his ID and boarding pass. "Except in his own mind. But Seth hit him so hard, Peele's helmet flew off. The mask cut his lip and he still has a scar."

"Wow," Troy said. "Seth's a hard hitter."

"No one knows if Peele tried to get the job in Atlanta because of that, but ever since he got it, he's written bad things about Seth every chance he's had," Kenny said, taking his ID back from the ticket agent. "It got really nasty at the end of last season when Seth was having a bad time with his knees. I don't know if you read any of it."

"Yeah, but who cares what some guy writes?" Troy said. "Peele never even made it in college football."

"It hurts," Kenny said. "Plus, it can cost you money. Teams read that stuff. It almost cost Seth his job, to be honest."

The line started to move.

"Well, buddy, I'm heading in," Kenny said. "You sure you're okay?"

"Yeah," Troy said, "the desk is right there. Thanks for the ride."

"Next time you'll ride up front, with me," Kenny said, giving Troy a wink as he headed for the metal detector.

Troy watched the announcer for a second, then turned and searched for his mom, but he didn't see her. He swam the length of the Delta desk through a sea of travelers, scanning their faces but seeing no sign of his mom. He looked up at the monitor. The clock in the corner said 8:23. Troy knew the team's charter flight was scheduled to take off at 8:30. He bit into his lip and swiveled his head from side to side the way he did when he played quarterback and the other team blitzed him. If he couldn't find his mom, he had no idea what he'd do.

He looked at the clock: 8:25. He began to run back and forth like a mouse caught in a cage.

There was no sign of his mother anywhere.

From within the packed crowd of people, a hand shot out, snatched his parka, and jerked him to a stop.

Startled, Troy looked up into the angry red face of a man with thinning blond hair and blue eyes. From one nostril of his sharp nose extended a white scar that tugged at his delicate pink lip.

"Who are you?" Troy asked, trying to break the grip that only got tighter.

CHAPTER FOUR

SHARP INCISOR TEETH SHOWED themselves in a mean smile as the man said, "I'm Brent Peele with the *Atlanta Journal-Constitution*. Who are you?"

Peele emerged from the crowd, tall and thin like a crane bird, with pants short enough to show the black socks he wore with his sneakers.

"How'd you get here?" Troy asked, unable to contain the question.

"I'm a reporter," Peele said. "I've got my ways."

Dipping his face down toward Troy's, he asked, "So, how is it you help the Falcons steal the other team's plays?"

"What are you talking about?" Troy said. He looked around for help but saw only fast-moving adults in overcoats hurrying for their planes.

"This team makes a turnaround too good to be true," Peele said, squinting, "and it *is* too good to be true. Same thing goes for Halloway. He was washed up last year, and all of a sudden people are talking Pro Bowl. He's no faster or stronger, same broken-down knees, but now he's always in the right place at the right time. Gee, how does that happen?"

"I don't know what you're talking about," Troy said, squirming to get away.

"Do you read the coaches' lips?" Peele asked. "What, you hack into the frequency on their quarterback radio?"

"You're nuts," Troy said.

"Where's your father?" Peele asked, looking around without loosening his grip.

Troy's throat tightened. He had no father, not one he knew, anyway. His mother didn't talk much about the man who had abandoned them before Troy was born. This left Troy with a vague feeling of hatred for his father, but what bothered him even more was the contradictory feeling of wanting to one day find the man and impress him. So disturbing were these feelings that even the mention of his father by a stranger—someone he didn't even care about—cut Troy deep.

"Leave me alone!" Troy shouted.

"Easy now," Peele said, softening his voice. "You're just a kid. You're not doing anything wrong here, but the team is. I know just what they're doing, trying to keep people from suspecting by using a kid."

"You're crazy," Troy said, loud enough to make a few people glance at him on their way past.

"Not quite," Peele said, lowering his voice even more, "and if you keep shouting, someone's going to call the police. I don't have a problem with that. I'm a reporter after a story. What's your explanation going to be?"

"It's a free country," Troy said.

"Not for kids," Peele said.

"Okay, okay," Troy said, going limp. "I'll take you to my dad. I'm supposed to meet him at the American Airlines desk."

"American?" Peele said, frowning. "That's in another terminal."

"Well, I don't know," Troy said, raising his shoulders before dropping them.

"Come on," Peele said. "This way."

Troy let the reporter steer him toward an escalator, riding it down with him. All the while Troy studied the signs to remember where everything was. Peele took him through a tunnel and up another set of escalators to the platform for the train that ran to the American Airlines terminal.

"You want to tell me how much they're paying you?" Peele asked, his tone smooth and oily.

Troy shrugged and said, "My dad will know."

"You live in Atlanta?" Peele asked as the train groaned into the station. Its doors banged open, and a computerized voice told everyone to get on.

"Not really," Troy said, quickly taking a seat facing the doors.

Peele sat down next to him but kept a hand on the right sleeve of Troy's parka. Troy unzipped the coat and wormed his left arm out of its sleeve.

The instant the doors beeped and started to shut, Troy stamped on the arch of Peele's foot, flew out of the parka, and launched himself toward the closing doors.

CHAPTER FIVE

TROY DIDN'T STOP TO WATCH the train. He sprinted down the escalator and back through the tunnel into the Delta terminal and up again to the counter, turning this way and that in search of his mom.

He walked the length of the counter and had just started back toward the other end when he heard his name above the noise of the crowded terminal. He spun and saw a hand waving frantically above people's heads.

"Mom!" he shouted.

She broke through the mob and hugged him tight. "Are you okay?"

Troy glanced at the clock: 8:42.

"The plane," he said. "Did it wait?"

"Maybe. Are you okay?"

"That guy grabbed me," Troy said, explaining what happened as they sprinted, hand in hand, through the terminal.

His mom flashed him a grin when he told her about stomping on Peele's instep and she said, "You did good."

As soon as Troy and his mom reached the security gate, a Delta supervisor in a red blazer and a TSA agent hustled them past the line and down several back hallways until they were outside in the foggy light of the tarmac. The smell of spent fuel turned Troy's stomach, and he plugged his ears against the scream of jet engines as they dashed across the grooved concrete. The Delta 727 charter sat by itself, away from the terminals. The team buses were chugging away, adding black clouds of diesel to the stench.

Troy pointed to the stairway being tugged free from the plane by a small tractor and said, "They're leaving."

His mom said nothing but dragged him toward the tail of the plane, where a narrow set of stairs still remained, like a forgotten toilet paper streamer. They dashed for the stairs, but with about twenty feet to go, the steps began to slowly retract into the tail of the plane. Troy's mom shouted and grabbed for the railing.

A flight attendant hollered something at her from inside the plane above them.

"We're with the team!" Troy's mom shouted.

The flight attendant's mouth dropped open. She pushed a different button and the stairs began to grind back down. Troy's mom leaped up the steps, and he followed.

"I'm sorry," the flight attendant said. "I thought we were supposed to leave without you."

"The terminal was swamped," Troy's mom said.

Seth was sitting only a couple seats from the back, wearing jeans, cowboy boots, and a white button-down shirt. The other players around him, big men who spilled over the edges of their seats and into the aisle, were already playing cards with one another. Seth set down his Coke and hustled into the galley, where Troy and his mom stood.

"Peele thinks we're stealing the other teams' plays when they make their calls," Troy said.

"Peele probably thinks he can win himself a Pulitzer Prize if he breaks a story and convinces people we're stealing plays," Seth said. "And if he can somehow ruin me in the process, all the better for him. The guy hates me."

Troy said in a soft voice, "But we're not cheating. Why can't we just tell Peele it's me? That I know the plays from watching what they did before. That there's a pattern. Tell him it's the same thing that every team does with computers when they study game film to learn the other teams' tendencies? Tell him I'm like this football 'genius.'"

"He'll laugh," his mom said. "He's not going to believe us."

"I can *show* him," Troy said, his face growing warm. "No one believes me until I show them."

"Except that Mr. Langan wants this to stay quiet, remember?" Seth said. "That's part of the deal. If he knows Peele is on to us, he might just shut the whole thing down."

The pilot's voice came on the loudspeaker and told everyone to find their seats and buckle in because they were cleared for takeoff.

Troy's mom said, "I better get up there with the rest of the staff. I won't say anything until we get a chance to talk more after we land."

Even though Troy's mom and Seth were a serious couple, they tried not to let anyone on the team—players or front office people—know about it. Troy's mom had gotten the job with the team on her own, before she even knew Seth, and she didn't want people to think anything different. So she sat up with the rest of the team's front office employees. Troy, however, as a "ball boy" and well liked by everyone, got to sit in the players' section.

"We can't let Peele stop us," Troy said to Seth after his mom had gone and the two of them sat in their own row, with an empty seat between them. "We can make the playoffs if we keep going. That's what everyone wants, especially Mr. Langan."

"They want that, yes," Seth said, "but they don't want trouble to come along with it."

"I thought teams did anything to win," Troy said.

"Some do," Seth said, "but not Mr. Langan. He doesn't have to win. He wants to win, but it's not going to make or break him if we do or don't. What he doesn't want is anything to hurt his reputation. That's even more important to him than winning."

"How would I hurt his reputation?" Troy asked, buckling his seat belt as the plane lurched forward. "What if I can prove to Peele that what we're doing isn't wrong?"

Troy remembered a time when no one except his grandfather believed him. It was only after he proved he could predict what plays the other team would run that the Falcons had let him help them win their last several games.

"No. I'm sorry, Troy. People will twist this around," Seth said as they rolled toward the runway. "Especially someone like Peele."

Troy clamped his mouth shut tight, thinking about what Seth said. The plane's engines began to roar. They lifted off the ground and an air pocket buffeted them sideways. Troy's stomach flipped, and he dug his fingers into the armrest of his seat.

"But he can't say it's wrong when it isn't," Troy finally said. "I'm not doing anything wrong!"

"Buddy," Seth said, looking over at him with a funny

smile, "welcome to the NFL. They don't have to write the truth. They just want to sell papers. As soon as Peele can prove you're involved with calling the defensive plays, he'll be able to blow it up into a huge scandal. It'll be ten times worse than that mess with the Patriots filming the Rams' practice before the Super Bowl. No one is going to believe you can do what we know you can do. The damage will be done before the real truth ever comes out. It'll be the end for you, me, my career, and probably your mom's job, too."

CHAPTER SIX

"WHAT DO YOU MEAN, no football practice?" Tate asked on Monday, pounding a fist on the lunch table and glaring at Troy with her big brown eyes. "This is the *playoffs*, the semifinals. We win Saturday and we go to the *state championship*. We have to practice."

Troy stuffed the rest of his ham sandwich into his mouth, chewed, and said, "My mom called the office, and we have to meet with Mr. Langan at seven o'clock tonight. Me, my mom, and Seth, too. It's important," Troy added, thinking about the ten thousand dollars a week the team was supposed to pay him, Seth's career, and his mom's job.

"Well, we can't have practice without our star quarterback and our head coach," Nathan said, filling his own mouth with Doritos and crunching loudly. Nathan was the biggest kid in Troy's grade and the anchor of the Duluth Tigers' line. Troy and Tate also played for the junior league team.

Jamie Renfro, a tall boy with dark curly hair, stopped behind Nathan with a lunch tray in his hands.

"*Star* quarterback?" Jamie said with a mean smile. "You guys are a joke. You got lucky just to be *in* the playoffs, and even luckier to steal a couple games, but your luck just ran out. The Dunwoody Dragons are going to eat you for a snack on Saturday."

"Snack on this," Nathan said, opening his mouth to reveal a smelly glob of chewed-up Doritos, letting it fall into his open palm, and offering it up to Jamie.

Jamie's eyes went wide and he retched like he might throw up.

"You're sick," Jamie said, walking away with a hand on his stomach.

"He's just jealous," Tate said, watching Jamie go, "but you are kind of sick."

"So? His dad shouldn't have quit as our coach before the last regular-season game," Nathan said as the glob slipped from his hand and plopped to the floor.

"Gross," Tate said.

Nathan's eyes went wide. He ran a hand over the stubble of his crew cut, scooped up the blob, and popped it back into his mouth with the rest of the mess.

"Two-second rule," Nathan said, talking through his

food, this time keeping it in his mouth.

"Two-second rule?" Tate said.

Troy shook his head and said, "If it's not on the floor for more than two seconds, you can pick it up and eat it."

"I think I'm going to be sick," Tate said, her face rumpled in disgust.

"It's a good thing Mr. Renfro did quit," Troy said. "Otherwise Seth wouldn't be our coach and we wouldn't have beaten anyone. We *were* lucky to get into the playoffs when Norcross got disqualified, but after that, it's been all Seth."

"And you, too," Tate said. "Seth changed things around and made us a lot better, but Jamie couldn't have thrown all the touchdown passes you've thrown in the past three weeks. Good thing he walked away with his dad."

"It's been *all* of us," Troy said to Tate. "You're the best kicker in the state, and Nathan's a monster."

"I like that," Nathan said, grinning large. "*The Monster.* Did you guys know that this is the first time Duluth has ever had a team make it this far?"

"That's why there's been, like, two thousand people at our games," Tate said. "Everyone's talking about us. We win Saturday and we get to play for the championship. You want to be a champ, don't you?"

"Sheesh, I've never been a champ in anything," Nathan said, running his hand over his crew cut again.

"How come you can't meet with Mr. Langan earlier?"

"He stayed in Chicago on business," Troy said. "He won't be back until seven. My mom and Seth are pretty nervous about this Peele guy."

On the bus ride to school that morning, Troy had already told them everything that happened over the weekend, filling in the blanks while walking the halls between classes.

"I think it would be awesome to have this guy do a big spread on you in the newspaper," Nathan said. "Maybe a color photo or something? Fame is fame. Look at all the pop stars."

"Nathan," Tate said, quiet, but serious, "half the pop stars' lives are like train wrecks."

"Well, they drive nice cars," Nathan said.

Tate rolled her eyes.

"It's just one practice," Troy said. "It won't kill us."

"But the Dunwoody Dragons might kill us," Tate said. "I heard Jamie talking in gym class right before lunch. His cousin plays on that team. He's six feet tall."

"Six feet?" Nathan said through his food.

"If he's as bad as Jamie, we'll be all set," Troy said.

"If he's as mean as Jamie and that big and he plays on their defensive line," Nathan said, "you better be ready to scramble."

"You're not going to protect me?" Troy asked. "What is that?"

"I'll try—hit him low in the knees—but six feet?

Sheesh," Nathan said, swiping his hand over his bristles of hair.

"I'm more worried about our playbook," Tate said, "and Jamie's father giving it to the Dunwoody coaches."

"Our playbook?" Troy said, alarmed. "That's cheating. Even with Seth changing things up, we use the same number system, and half the plays we run I call at the line. If they get our playbook, we won't stand a chance. He wouldn't do that."

"Oh?" Tate said, raising her eyebrows. "Wouldn't he? Wait till I tell you what else I heard."

CHAPTER SEVEN

TROY AND NATHAN LEANED toward her.

"Sara Parks told Jamie in front of everyone that he and his dad were rotten to root for Dunwoody when we all live in Duluth," Tate said. "So then Jamie went all red, told her that his dad made the playbook and he could do what he wanted with it. He said if Seth Halloway wanted to have a team, he could make up his own playbook."

"But Seth has us running some new plays," Nathan said.

"We run a lot of old ones, though," Troy said, scowling and balling up the cellophane from his sandwich. "You can't learn all new plays in a week or two. *He's* the one who quit on the team.

"We'll have to change our calls. It'll be like learning

a whole new language. If we don't, they'll know where the ball is going every time we call a play at the line."

Nathan frowned and said, "Yeah, didn't you call the play at the line last week on, like, every touchdown?"

"That's because he can read the defenses," Tate said. "Have you been paying attention to everything going on here for the past month? The Falcons hired him because he can predict plays. He knows what the other team is going to do."

"That's in the NFL, though," Nathan said, scratching at his crew cut.

"Football is football," Tate said.

"Sheesh, now I got a girl telling me about football," Nathan said, plastering his hand over his face.

"Not just a girl," Troy said. "A girl who won the punt, pass, and kick contest against the boys, and a girl who kicked the winning field goal that got us into the playoffs after some big lug—I won't say his name—got a holding penalty that kept us out of the end zone."

"Hey, that was an aggressive mistake," Nathan said.

"Don't worry," Tate said to Troy, "he doesn't mean it."

"How could somebody be that low?" Troy asked.

"Who's low?" Nathan said.

"No, not you," Troy said. "I'm talking about Mr. Renfro giving our playbook away."

"Because the only person who hates you more than Jamie Renfro," Tate said, "is his father."

"And I bet he hates Seth even more," Nathan said.

"Like you said," Troy said, "he shouldn't have quit the team."

"He thought he was getting back at us by making us forfeit after Tate's mom complained to the league about all his screaming and yelling," Nathan said, "but we got the last laugh."

"Then let's work on it after school," Tate said. "We can go through the plays we run the most and start changing the names. And Troy, you can change the hot calls. We can write it all down and give it to Seth so he doesn't have to worry about it. He can just coach us on the football stuff."

"Great idea," Troy said, smiling at her. "We can go to my house."

"And I'll make the dip," Nathan said.

"Dip?" Troy asked.

"For chips and dip," Nathan said. "I love those blue corn things your mom buys, and I got a new recipe: sour cream, garlic, chives, and Tabasco sauce. A man's gotta eat, you know."

When the school bus dropped them off, Troy and his friends walked the long dirt road to the small saltbox house where he lived with his mom, in a stand of towering pines by the railroad tracks. The gritty red clay lot in front where his mom parked the car stood empty except for a scattering of pine needles too stubborn for the wind. The old tire Troy used as a target for throwing footballs drifted gently back and forth in the pleasant November breeze, and the sky overhead blinded them with the brilliance of its blue.

Inside, Troy raided the fridge for sodas and Nathan made what he'd begun calling his "famous" dip. Together they completed the changes to the playbook by the time Troy's mom returned home from work. She looked tired, but she smiled and talked to Nathan and Tate, offering them more sodas as if she hadn't a care in the world. After a few minutes, Troy's friends left, circling around back where a path led down through the pines to the tracks that allowed them to walk a straight shot to the Pine Grove Apartments, where they both lived.

When they'd gone, Troy's mom slumped down at the kitchen table and let go a sigh.

"What's going on?" Troy asked.

"I hate to lie, that's all," his mom said, dropping her face into one hand and rubbing her eyes. "In the morning, I set up interviews about the potential playoff run and how Coach McFadden's job might be saved. I didn't even see Peele. Then, about an hour after lunch, he showed up, limping around and talking about a kid who he knows is with the team who stomped on his foot. I told him I had nothing more to say."

Troy studied his mom, her long hair pulled back into a ponytail, her thin fingers curled around the edges of her pretty face. He knew her well, just as she knew him well, so instead of asking, he just waited. Finally, she spoke.

"So, of course," she said, "Peele went to my boss, Cecilia Fetters."

"And she doesn't know about me, right?"

"No," his mom said, "she thinks you're a ball boy like everyone else outside the players and coaches, and that's why I feel so bad, because I *hate* to lie."

"But if you told Mr. Langan you wouldn't say anything about me to anyone, then you couldn't break your promise to him," Troy said.

"So, I lied," his mom said, "which I hate to do."

"I guess sometimes you kind of have to," Troy said.

His mom shook her head.

"Just when everything was going great for you, me, and Seth," Troy said, slumping down in a chair beside her. "The Falcons on a playoff run? The Tigers in the semifinals of the state championship? Now this mess, and we've got to meet with Mr. Langan when we should be practicing. Why does some reporter have to ruin it all?"

His mom just kept slowly shaking her head, then perked up suddenly and said, "Oh, I forgot. Here."

From her purse, she removed a long white envelope and handed it to Troy.

"What is it?"

"Look inside," she said. "I know *this* will cheer you up."

CHAPTER EIGHT

TROY WORMED HIS FINGER into the opening and split open the envelope. He fished out the check and sucked in his breath.

The numbers jumped out at him.

Ten thousand dollars.

"Wow," he said, glancing up at his mom and sharing her smile. "It's real."

"Of course it's real," his mom said. "That's why I wanted you to see it instead of doing that direct deposit thing."

Troy had already earned twenty thousand dollars for the first two games he worked, but the money had gone straight into his bank account.

"I like seeing it like this!" he said. "That's a lot of zeros and a lot of money."

"And not a bad deal for the team, either," his mom said. "Ten thousand dollars per win? People would pay a lot more."

"You think we should ask for more?" Troy asked.

"No, I'm just saying," she said. "A deal's a deal. The whole thing is pretty unusual. I'm just glad Mr. Langan agreed to try it out."

"But this will be gone, too," Troy said. "If Peele messes everything up."

"That won't be gone," she said. "That's yours, and we're putting it in the bank with the rest of it. You earned it, and no one can take it away. That can pay for two or three years of college at a nice state school if we invest it right. After a couple more weeks, your education will be taken care of, Troy. It's a big thing. It's worth a little trouble along the way, believe me."

Troy studied the number, thinking of everything his mom had done for him without the help of a husband, then looked up at her and said, "I thought maybe you could do something with the money, Mom. I'm gonna get a football scholarship. I won't need this. I thought maybe you could buy yourself a new car, or even get a bigger house."

Troy's mom reached out and gripped his hand. Her eyes got shiny and a small smile bloomed on her face.

"You are so sweet," she said quietly, "but I don't need anything. This house, it's small, but I like it."

"I like it, too," Troy said. "I didn't mean that, but

you deserve it. I see other moms with expensive cars and diamonds and all that. Jamie Renfro's mom drives around in a Jaguar and she doesn't even have a job. You're the best. I should get you things."

"Honey, I don't care what car I drive or jewelry I wear," his mom said, holding up her other hand. "I appreciate you thinking of me, but we'll save this for college, in case you get a knee injury or something and the football thing doesn't work out. Or even if it does, you can buy a car for yourself. Believe it or not, it won't be long before you'll want one."

"Will you let me get you all that stuff if I sign a big NFL contract?" Troy asked.

She smiled and messed his hair. "Okay, that's a deal."

Troy grinned and said, "Maybe I'll save up for a Mustang. How much is a Mustang, anyway?"

"More than thirty thousand," his mom said, standing. "Let's get going. We can stop on the way and have a burger or pizza or something."

"How about I buy?" Troy said, waggling his eyebrows and snapping the check.

Troy liked Whoppers with cheese, and that's what they had before heading out to the Falcons complex. Seth was still there; he'd spent the afternoon getting treatment on his bad knee and lifting weights, and he met them at the side entrance where the staff and players came and went. He wore street clothes, but two bags of ice had been wrapped with an Ace bandage around the outside of his jeans. Troy's mom handed Seth a bag of cheeseburgers, and he started eating one as they walked through the halls and upstairs to the executive offices.

Action photographs of the team's star players lined the walls. In one, Seth stared out at them, his eyes wide, his mouth twisted into a snarl behind the metal cage of his face mask.

"Doesn't even look like you," Troy said, pointing up at the picture. "Too mean."

Seth widened his green eyes and bared his teeth, growling.

"Better," Troy said, laughing.

"Live clean, play mean," Seth said, letting his face return to its normal mask of pleasant calm.

Angie, Mr. Langan's assistant, showed them into the owner's office, sitting them down on the leather couch and telling them she expected Mr. Langan any minute. Seth spread his food out on the coffee table and kept digging into the burgers, washing them down with a bottle of water.

"I almost forgot," Troy said, tugging a folded piece of notebook paper from his pocket and handing it to Seth. "Jamie Renfro has a cousin who plays for Dunwoody. We heard his dad is giving them our playbook."

"You're kidding," Seth said.

Troy shook his head. "Tate and Nathan and I

renamed our plays and all the hot routes, even the stunts on the defensive line."

"So they won't know what we're doing," Seth said, studying the piece of paper. "This is great."

Troy grinned at his mom. Seth ate and nodded as he studied their work. He was just wiping his mouth on a napkin and stuffing the last of his garbage into the bag when Mr. Langan came through the door. He shook hands with them all, including Troy, before sitting down in a leather wingback chair and crossing his legs. The owner's hair was short, neatly cut, and sprinkled with gray. His tan, lean face had a pleasant, almost sleepy look, except for the green eyes, as churning and alive as whirlpools.

"Where are we?" he asked.

As Troy's mom explained what had happened, Mr. Langan's face remained impassive. The only expression that disturbed it was a small smile and a flicker of his eyes when he heard about Troy stomping Peele's foot.

When she finished, he made a steeple of his fingertips and rested them against his mouth. Finally, he broke the steeple and said, "I was afraid of this."

"None of us said anything," Seth said.

Mr. Langan shook his head and said, "No, I didn't think you would, and I'm sure coaches McFadden and Mora didn't say anything, either. They have more to gain from this than anyone. I just didn't know how long we could go before someone started asking questions.

You know when the Bears ran that slant play at the end of the game? The ball's snapped and you just run right to the spot before the receiver even gets there and you pick it off? Well, that kind of jumps out at people."

"I've made plenty of plays just like that," Seth said.

Mr. Langan considered him a moment before he said, "Ten years ago, you made those plays. But that's neither here nor there. Peele suspects something, and we have to deal with it. What I want to do is keep this under wraps as long as we can. We need to figure out a way to get Troy's input during the game *without* him being on the sideline."

"That's easy," Seth said. "We did that before, when we played the Raiders."

"Yes, you did," Mr. Langan said, "but no one was looking for Troy then. This will be different. Peele's not dumb."

"But Peele thinks we're somehow stealing the plays from the other team," Troy's mom said. "He thinks Troy is just the way we get the message to Coach Mora, not how we get the message about *what to do*."

"So if we take Troy out of the equation," the owner said, "Peele will have to find evidence that we're stealing the other teams' plays. Since we're not doing that, he's out of luck. If we keep Troy out of Peele's way, he'll never figure out what we're doing."

"But Mr. Langan," Troy said, his voice bursting with frustration, "we're not doing anything *wrong*."

"But we're doing something different," Mr. Langan said, "something people are going to have a hard time explaining, and, believe it or not, doing something *different* scares people and gets them a lot more riled up than doing something *wrong*. People do the wrong thing every day.

"As long as we can keep Peele from finding out that you are our football genius, we can just keep marching toward the playoffs."

"What if he does find out?" Troy said, unable to keep from asking the question. He couldn't help thinking of Nathan's words about Peele doing a big spread on him in the newspaper—about fame and pop stars and the nice cars that famous people drive. Tate's voice came into his mind as well, talking about their lives being train wrecks, but that wasn't true about *everyone* famous. Some famous people had it all, and lots of famous people were loved by everyone, even people they didn't know.

Maybe even a father they didn't know.

Mr. Langan returned the steeple of fingers to his mouth for a minute before he looked at Troy and said, "If Peele can prove you're helping us call the plays, then we'll go to the NFL and see what they think."

"That's not so bad," Troy's mom said.

Mr. Langan gave a painful smile and said, "It's not good, either, though. First of all, we would have to stop using Troy while the league figures out how they want to handle it, and second, while they might not say we've done anything wrong, I know my fellow owners pretty well. If we've got something that helps us win, something that they don't have? Even if it's not against the rules? They might make up some new rules."

"So we're okay as long as Troy doesn't get caught?" Seth asked.

"That's right," Mr. Langan said. "Just don't get caught."

CHAPTER NINE

TROY'S SEMIFINAL GAME on Saturday came fast. Seth worked the Tigers extra hard the remaining nights that week. The rest of the team picked up on the new calls Troy would be making at the line so that if the Dragons really did have the team's playbook, the Tigers would be ready. And still, Troy wished he had even more time to prepare. This would be the biggest game he'd ever played in, and the need to win it crept through his bones like the ache from a fever.

"These guys can't be seventh graders," Nathan said, peering across the field at the Dunwoody Dragons in their all-red uniforms.

"They look like a high school team," Tate said, removing her helmet and shaking loose her long dark hair.

Troy didn't say anything. He just stared and blinked,

thinking that maybe the bright sunshine gleaming off their bloodred helmets might somehow be creating an optical illusion, making the Dragons look twice the size they really were.

"Don't worry," Seth said, stepping into their midst and tapping the rolled-up paper that was their game plan against the palm of his free hand. "We've got a plan."

"Better plan on lots of ice and ibuprofen," Nathan said. "Sheesh."

"You can block them, Nathan," Seth said. "Just hit them low."

"I'd have to be seven feet tall to hit them high," Nathan said.

"Every pass play we run is going to be a roll-out," Seth said, "so you just trip them up. Troy's faster than any of those defensive linemen, and he can throw on the run."

"Are we going to use any running plays at all?" Troy asked.

Seth shaded his eyes from the sun, squinting across the field at the Dragons. He cringed and shook his head. "I don't think that would be a good idea. Go on, they're calling the captains for the coin toss. You three get out there and give us some luck."

Their cleats sunk into the fresh turf, kicking up the warm smell of dirt and cut grass to mix with the scent of popcorn, hot dogs, and burgers cooking in the concession stand. The Dragons' three captains stood nearly as tall as the referees, and the one Troy figured to be Jamie Renfro's cousin was actually taller than three of the five adults. When Troy shook their hands, the cousin clamped down on Troy's fingers and flashed him a wicked smile. Troy snatched his hand away and sneered right back.

They flipped the coin. Nathan chose tails. It came up heads.

"How about best two out of three?" Nathan asked the ref.

The ref curled his lip and said, "What are you talking about? No."

Nathan said, "You can't blame a guy for trying."

As they parted from the middle of the field, Troy felt someone tug his arm. He turned to see Jamie's enormous cousin glaring at him through the bars of his face mask.

"We'll see how bad you want to play quarterback after I mash your bones," he said in a nasty whisper that the refs couldn't hear.

Seth rallied the team together in a tight circle and said, "Look at you guys. All I see is a bunch of kids ready to lay down and get beat. Well, that's not going to happen. You guys got to realize where you are. We win this and we're playing under the lights for the *Georgia state championship* on TV! Do you realize how many great athletes work their entire lives and never win a championship? It's something no one can ever take away from you, but you got to go get it! I don't care how big they are. You got to take it from them!"

Seth's face turned red and his chiseled jaw rippled with intensity. He stabbed his finger at the other sideline with the thick muscles in his arm bulging.

"But you're bigger than everyone," Tate said quietly.

Seth's face softened.

"Not when I play I'm not," he said, shaking his head. "I'm as small on an NFL field as you are against these guys. It's not all about size. It's about here and here."

Seth pointed to the center of his own chest, then his head.

"Heart and brains," he said, pulling the game plan out of his back pocket and brandishing it at them like a kid showing off a straight-A report card. "Me and your team captains? We got the brains part handled, but *you* guys got to have the heart. You gotta believe we can beat them, and I promise you, we will.

"Now, bring it in here and let's hear it: 'Heart' on three. Ready? One, two, three—"

"Heart!"

The word echoed through Troy's skull. They broke the circle, and the kickoff team jogged out onto the field. Troy paced the sideline, willing the Tigers' kickoff team to hold. Behind them, hundreds of fans from Duluth cheered and waved the blue and gold pom-poms Troy's mom and the other moms had handed out to relatives, friends, and Duluth football fans. On the other side, a sea of red, twice the size of the Tigers fans, roared while performing a sweeping wave. Troy shuddered at the demonic sound the Dunwoody fans called their Dragon Roar.

Tate kicked the ball to start the game. End over end it sailed, high and far. The Dragons' runner had to retreat ten yards to field it, but when he did, he turned on a jet of speed that left the Tigers' defenders zigging in his zags. When the Dragons' runner crossed the fifty, Nathan threw himself at his feet. The runner hurdled Nathan easily. Only Tate now stood between the runner and the end zone. Instead of trying to avoid Tate the way he had the other Tigers' defenders, the runner lowered his shoulder and churned straight at her, looking to mangle her and plow her over on his way to a touchdown.

Tate, thin as a wisp of smoke but wiry and quick, darted forward with her arms spread wide, straight at the oncoming freight train.

Troy flinched and waited for the Dragon Roar.

CHAPTER TEN

TATE LAUNCHED HERSELF LIKE a javelin at the runner's knees, upending him so that he somersaulted through the air, landing on his back with a thud Troy could practically feel.

The cheers came from the Tigers fans.

Tate sprang up off the grass and left the Dragons' runner lying in a heap, twisting from side to side. As the Tigers' battered kickoff team jogged to the benches, the Dragons' coaches helped the runner to his feet and tugged him off the field.

The Tigers' defense took the field with a war cry, half of them stopping along the way to high five Tate.

"That was incredible, Tate!" Seth said, slapping her shoulder pad. "You just saved a touchdown."

"Hey," Tate said, grinning from ear to ear, "I'm not

just a kicker. I'm a football player."

Troy slapped her five and told her she was awesome. Together they watched their defense take on the Dragons' offense. Nathan, who played both ways, battled it out with the Dragons' massive offensive line, sometimes even breaking into the backfield. But their size was too much for the rest of the defense, and it took the Dragons only six plays to march forty-four yards into the end zone and set off a Dragon Roar loud enough to make Troy cover his ears.

"Look," Tate said, pointing toward the top row of the Dragons bleachers.

Troy followed the line of her finger and saw a big man and a tall boy with dark curly hair, each of them dressed in red, cheering with the rest of the Dunwoody crowd: Jamie Renfro and his father.

"The rats," Troy said.

Seth came up from behind, put an arm around Troy, and said, "It's gonna have to be a shoot-out."

"What's a shoot-out?" Tate asked.

"Both teams score every time they touch the ball," Seth said. "Whoever has the ball last wins."

"We have to score every time?" Troy asked.

Seth pressed his lips tight, then lowered his voice and said, "Unless we get a turnover, I can't see how our defense is going to stop them. The good news is that I know you can do it."

The energy in Seth's voice went through Troy like an

electric current, and as he ran out onto the field after the kickoff, he believed he really could do it.

Because they were going to call all the plays at the line, the Tigers' offense didn't bother to huddle. The "no-huddle" offense would put extra pressure on the defense, making it harder for them to get plays signaled in from the sideline and to make adjustments to different formations. Troy knew the no-huddle offense would cut down on the Dragons' ability to run complicated blitzes.

Hopeful, Troy lined up behind the center and called out his first play as part of the cadence.

"Red Tango 17," he said, barking out the signals above the noise from the crowd. "Red Tango 17 . . ."

The Dragons' defensive backs and linebackers crept up toward the line of scrimmage and shifted to the left, expecting the Tigers to run there. Troy broke out into a huge grin. It was all he could do to keep from laughing with joy.

He knew now for certain that Jamie Renfro's father *had* given the playbook to the Dragons. But the *new* Red Tango 17 play would send Rusty Howell, the Tigers' fastest man, straight down the field for a pass.

"Hut!" Troy said. "Hut! Hut!"

He took the snap and rolled to his right. Nathan and the rest of the Tigers' line chopped at the defenders' knees but slowed them only a little. The enormous Dragons surged toward Troy in a wave. He ran for his life toward the sideline. Rusty sprinted downfield, passing the defenders who raced toward Troy thinking the play was a run.

Just as the red wave of defenders was about to crash down on Troy, he set his feet and fired the ball.

CHAPTER ELEVEN

TROY WATCHED THE BALL'S flight and Rusty racing toward the end zone with his arms stretched. The thought that maybe he'd thrown it too far flickered in Troy's mind, only to be snuffed out—along with everything else—when the Dragons' linemen swamped him.

"I cut my guy down like a blade of grass, but half the defense buried you and rang your bell," Nathan said, helping Troy to his feet.

"What happened?" Troy asked.

"With me blocking for you? Touchdown. What else?" Nathan said nonchalantly. "Can you hold for the kick?"

Troy wobbled a little on his feet but shook the cobwebs out of his head and started a slow jog down the field toward the end zone, where Tate was already setting up her tee for the extra point.

When Tate kicked it through to tie the score, the three of them ran off together, slapping high-fives and smacking shoulders with the rest of the team. Troy took off his helmet and pointed to Jamie Renfro up in the stands, grinning and giving him a big thumbs-up.

"Looks like his head is about ready to explode," Tate said, giggling when she saw what Troy was doing.

"Serves him right," Nathan said. "The traitor."

The game was indeed a shoot-out, with each team seeming to score on every possession, but the rest of the Tigers' touchdowns didn't come as easy as the first one. As the game wore on, the Dragons relied less and less on the plays they thought they knew and more and more on their superior size, strength, and speed. Still, Troy's ability to read the defense, some good play by the Tigers' receivers, Tate's sure leg, and Seth's strategy of having Troy throw on the run all worked. With less than a minute to go in the game, the Tigers were down by just seven points, 42–35.

Troy worked the offense down the field on what would be the last Tigers' possession. With only four seconds remaining, he hit Rusty in the end zone for a touchdown, making it 42–41.

The Dragons crowd went silent, and the Duluth fans pumped out a roar of their own that rose and fell in Troy's ears like ocean waves. But instead of celebrating with Rusty and his teammates in the end zone, Troy made a beeline for Seth, who wore a worried look.

Kicking the extra point would tie the game and send them into sudden-death overtime. If the Dragons won the coin toss, they'd likely score and win. The Tigers' other option was to go for a two-point conversion by either running or passing the ball into the end zone from the three-yard line. That would win the game by a point and send them to the Georgia state championship.

"What do we do?" Troy asked Seth, gritting his teeth so hard that his cheeks ached.

The NFL linebacker looked down at him and asked, "What do you think?"

"I don't want to win or lose on a coin flip," Troy said.

"We can't run it," Seth said. "They're too big. It'd have to be a short pass, but only the long passes have been working for us. I don't like our chances."

"Then let's fake the kick," Troy said. "Get them out of their regular defense."

Seth's face brightened and he grinned at Troy. "I love it."

Seth cupped his hands and yelled to his players, "Kicking team!"

"I'll roll right," Troy said, his heart hammering away now, "and send the ends up and to the right on different levels."

"Like two Ls," Seth said, nodding.

"Only I don't throw to them," Troy said. "That's something they might be ready for."

"You can't run it in," Seth said. "They'll have a safety on either side."

"I won't run it," Troy said.

The referee set the ball on the three-yard line and signaled Seth to get going.

"You're talking in riddles," Seth said, scowling.

"A throw back," Troy said. Everyone would go to the right, but they'd send just one player back to the left, a classic trick play.

"To who?" Seth asked.

"The kicker," Troy said.

CHAPTER TWELVE

"TATE? WELL, I DON'T call you a football genius for nothing," Seth said, grinning again and nodding. "They'll never pick it up. Go!"

Troy sprinted out to the huddle. As he went to the line, Troy couldn't help glancing up at Jamie Renfro. Like the rest of the Dragons crowd, the Renfros were on their feet. Troy wanted to win for a lot of reasons. He wanted to be a star player. He wanted to be noticed by coaches and college scouts. But he also wanted to show Jamie Renfro and his coach-dad how foolish it had been to sit Troy on the bench all season.

The fans in both bleachers cheered wildly now, and Troy had to shout. He drew the play in the grass for his teammates as he spoke, then looked at Tate.

"Tate," Troy said as loud as he could, looking into

her big dark eyes, "you fake the kick, actually swing your leg. I'll pull the ball at the last second and you take off into the end zone. They'll all come for me, and you'll be wide open."

"Me?" Tate said. Her eyes widened and glistened at him like glass.

"You can do it," Nathan said, slapping her shoulder pad.

Tate rolled her lower lip under her upper teeth but nodded.

Troy broke the huddle. They jogged to the line. Tate set her kicking tee down in the grass and marched off her steps. Troy knelt down over the tee and looked back at her.

Tate smiled weakly. Troy smiled back and winked with an affirmative nod. He turned and signaled for the snap. It came like a bullet. Troy snared it and rested it on the tee for a split second before pulling it up just as Tate swung her foot.

From the corner of his eye, Troy saw his line collapse and a blur of red surge at him like a typhoon. He tucked the ball, jumped up, spun around, and sprinted for the right side of the end zone. The Dragons came fast. The safeties covered the ends, sticking to them like glue, but that's where Troy kept his eyes, knowing that if he looked at Tate it might give the trick away.

He was nearly to the sideline with defenders all around him and no chance at running into the end zone before he cranked his hips and head around and set his feet to make the throw. He held it as long as he could, then launched it an instant before being buried in red. Little comets of light exploded across his field of vision, then went out. In the darkness at the bottom of the pile, Troy grunted in dismay.

When he'd let the ball go, Tate was nowhere to be seen.

CHAPTER THIRTEEN

AS HE FOUGHT HIS WAY up through the pile of bodies, Troy heard the explosion of cheers. He batted another arm off his face mask, stepped on someone's leg, and tripped forward out of the pile like a zombie breaking free from his grave.

There, in the end zone, atop the shoulders of the entire team, Tate sat with one hand holding up the ball and the other pointing a single finger to the sky. The scoreboard confirmed it for him. Somehow, from somewhere, Tate had caught his pass in the end zone for the two-point conversion. The Duluth fans poured over the fence, swarming the end zone. The Tigers were in the championship!

As Troy ran for the melee, Seth scooped him up, holding him by the waist, hollering and spinning him in a circle as he sliced into the middle of the Tigers players and fans. When they reached Tate, Nathan was already there, holding her up. Troy flung his arms around them both, hugging them and screaming with joy as they, and the players and coaches beneath them, collapsed into a pile of laughing, bellowing winners.

After a minute of mayhem, Seth's shouting could be heard by everyone and the team assembled in an orderly line behind Tate to cross the field and shake hands with the dejected Dragons. Afterward, Seth gathered the team by the Tigers bench, with the parents and fans staying back at a respectful distance. Troy and his teammates had to strain to hear Seth's voice, it was so hoarse and raspy from shouting.

"We won the North," Seth said, referring to one of the two regions in the state, "and that's an incredible accomplishment for a team that barely made the playoffs. But you believed, and now we go to the state championship. You believed and you had heart, and we're not done yet!"

The team cheered.

Seth held up his hands and the players gradually grew quiet.

"Next week, we're going to win it all," Seth said. "That's how I want you to think. We're going to enjoy a day off—I should say *you guys* will enjoy a day off; I've got to play a game against Seattle—and then we're going to prepare like no other team has ever prepared.

We're going to come up with a plan to beat the pants off whoever they send at us, however good they are, however big they are, however fast, however strong. We are the Tigers and we *will* be champions!"

CHAPTER FOURTEEN

WHEN THE CROWD FINALLY dispersed, Troy climbed into Seth's big yellow H2 along with his mom. His mind spun with the thought of being the quarterback of a state championship team. It would set him apart from his peers and put him on the track he ached for: the road to the NFL, not as a football genius, but as a real player. If Troy could win next week's game, high school coaches, college coaches, the media, other players, and fans would rally around him in the years to come, giving him every advantage he could hope for. He would be marked as a champion.

The thought of that made Troy worry, though, because it was at moments like this throughout his life—just when everything seemed to be going great—that things turned sour instead.

Troy knew Seth was headed to Wright's Gourmet for their favorite sandwiches, but on the way, he pulled into a newly constructed shopping center where half the glass storefronts were still plastered with real estate ads. Only a handful of cars rested in the smooth parking lot, and most of them were at the far end, in front of a Fantastic Fitness Center marked by its big red neon sign. In the middle of the shopping center was a large steakhouse that appeared to open only for dinner.

"What's this?" Troy asked, eyeing the fogged glass of the storefront on the near end of the brick shopping center.

"A little unorthodox medical treatment," Seth said. "A vitamin shot and an adjustment. It won't take long."

Troy scrunched up his face.

His mom said, "A lot of the players get things like acupuncture and vitamin shots and back adjustments."

"Players and old people looking for the fountain of youth," Seth said, getting out of the truck.

"Well," Troy said, "if I'm going to play in the NFL one day, maybe I should check it out."

"Come in if you want," Seth said.

Troy's mom said, "I hate to drive this thing, but I'm going to run across the street to the Kroger and get some orange juice. I'll meet you guys back here."

"Why do you hate it?" Seth asked, his voice still hoarse, as she scooted over into the driver's seat.

She shrugged and said, "It's a gas guzzler."

Seth scratched his head and said, “Well, I need some new wheels anyway. Maybe a hybrid truck.”

Troy’s mom tilted her head and smiled lovingly at Seth. Seth put a hand on her cheek and when Troy’s mom leaned over and kissed Seth, Troy blushed and looked away, climbing out of the truck and waiting on the curb with his eyes on the ground.

Seth hopped out and patted him on the back. Troy’s mom rumbled away, high up in the H2, and Troy followed Seth through the dark glass door whose fancy gold letters read MERCURY MEDICAL GROUP. Inside a small waiting room, two bulky black leather chairs rested on a thick gray rug with a brass lamp between them. Large prints of modern art paintings hung in chrome frames from the white walls. Troy sniffed at the new smell of the carpet, then folded his arms across his chest and shivered.

“Why’s it so cold in here?” he asked Seth.

Seth pointed to a big vent up by the ceiling and said, “The AC unit for the whole building is right over us. It has to pump hard to get all the way to the other end for Fantastic Fitness, so the doc’s place is always cold. It’s nice in the summer, though.”

Seth opened a heavy wooden door, went down a short hall, gave one knock, and went right into a large office where a man, surrounded by piles of papers and magazines, worked at a computer. Beneath his lab coat, he wore a bright green cardigan sweater over a white T-shirt. His tan skin had an orange tint to it. Three faded leg bones on his desk held down papers that rustled in the air blowing from a second AC vent directly above him.

Next to the desk, a skeleton hung from a chrome metal stand. Two detailed diagrams of the human body were plastered onto the wall behind it. On the far end of the room, an exam table stood amid an island of green marble, and shelves and counters of black granite lined the walls. The man, tall and thin with spidery brown hair on his arms and poking up from the collar of his white T-shirt, rounded the desk and extended a hand to Seth.

"Good to see you," he said, nodding so that long strands of bleached blond hair had to be swept back from his eyes—eyes so cold and blue that Troy felt like they could look right through him.

"Troy," Seth said, "this is Doc Gumble."

Troy shook the doctor's cold, damp hand.

"Hey, little fella. Uh," Gumble said, looking from Troy to Seth, "he's going to wait in the front, right?"

Seth frowned and looked at Troy. "He was interested in how this whole thing is done. I'm good with it if you are."

"Honestly? I think it's better if he waits out front," Gumble said, looking at Troy with cold, knowing eyes that made Troy happy to leave. "It's better. Really."

"Well, I'll be right out, buddy," Seth said, winking at

Troy. "You know, doctor's orders and all that."

Troy nodded and stepped outside. He was halfway down the hall when he heard two quick snaps that made him spin around. Worry froze him in his tracks and he returned, pushing his ear to the office door. The sickening sound made Troy wonder if the doctor hadn't broken Seth's neck. With his heart hammering, he turned the doorknob and opened it just a pinch. He rested his forehead on the door, angling it so that his eye was even with the crack, and held his breath.

Seth lay on the table with his head in both of Gumble's hands. The doctor was snapping it a second time, first one way, then the other, and Seth's vertebrae crackled like a bundle of dry sticks. Seth groaned, and Troy contorted his face. His stomach heaved and he turned away.

Without a sound, Troy closed the office door and hurried outside. He scanned the area for his mom and saw her pulling into the lot when he noticed a small silver car in front of the steakhouse. It hadn't been there before. In the front seat was a man whose face Troy couldn't quite make out because of the glare.

Troy's mom pulled up and beeped the horn, and by the time Troy circled the H2, the car had pulled out of its spot, heading for the exit. As it passed, it slowed, and the passenger window rolled down. The driver leaned across the seat and snapped a picture of Troy, then kept going.

Troy's mouth fell open and he blinked as the silver car screeched out of the parking lot. When the camera came away from the man's face, Troy recognized the driver.

Brent Peele.

Troy's mom rolled her window down and asked, "What's up?"

"Nothing," Troy said, wishing it were true.

CHAPTER FIFTEEN

WHEN SETH CAME OUT, he and Troy climbed into the H2. Troy opened his mouth to tell his mom and Seth about Peele, but it seemed too strange. It seemed like he'd dreamed the whole thing. Maybe his imagination was running away with him. Maybe one of the hits he'd taken during the game had left him confused. Maybe he was dehydrated or something. The doubt kept him quiet.

At Wright's Gourmet, Troy got his favorite: a Rebel Rueben with a piece of chocolate cake and a root beer to wash it down. He pushed the thought of Brent Peele out of his mind, and the three of them talked and laughed about the Tigers' victory. Troy's mom asked who they'd have to face for the state championship.

"The winner of the Valdosta Vipers and the Forest

Park Titans game," Troy said, looking up at the clock on the wall. "They're playing right now, right, Seth?"

"Yup," Seth said, taking a swig of his own root beer. "Valdosta's the favorite. They've won the state title three out of the last five years. But whoever it is, we're not going to have the advantage of them thinking they know our plays."

"But you said we can win this," Troy said. "That we can be the champs."

Seth offered him a grim smile and said, "Anyone can beat anyone, right? That's why you play. It's just that our defense, well, you saw what Dunwoody did to them."

Troy's mom crunched a BBQ chip and asked, "Why don't you do the same thing Troy does with the Falcons?"

Seth nodded his head and said, "I know. I'd like to, but the problem is that I don't have anyone who can learn the kind of signals you'd need to send in and make the calls at the line of scrimmage an instant before the other team snaps the ball. The offense that Coach Renfro put together is actually pretty good. The kids have enough good plays that I can just tinker with it a little and it's no big deal. But he didn't know anything about defense, and we just don't have time to teach all the kids a whole new system."

"What if Troy played defense?" his mom asked. "Could he learn it all?"

Seth twirled his soda bottle, thinking a moment before he nodded, looked up, and said, "Yes, I bet he could. Not only that, he'd know where the ball was going, so even if he couldn't get the rest of the defense in the right spot, we'd be a lot better off with him in there."

"So?" his mom said.

"He's never played defense," Seth said softly. "It's not something you just do. Most teams protect their quarterbacks, even in a junior league. If you have a good one, you can't afford to get him hurt. And I'm walking, or limping, proof that if you play defense, you're gonna get hurt."

"I could do it," Troy said. "Play safety or cornerback or something. I know all about pass coverage."

"I know you know it," Seth said. "And you're a good enough athlete that you could do it. But if we're gonna have you do it, we gotta get started."

"You don't mean right now?" Troy's mom said.

"Yes," Seth said, wiping his hands and standing up. "I do."

"Look at him, Seth," his mom said, extending her open hand at Troy. "He's tired and sore. He hasn't even had a shower."

"Yeah," Seth said, collecting the round baskets their food came in, dumping their trash, and grinning at Troy's mom, "it's a rough way to make a living. I wouldn't advise it for anyone."

Troy spent what was left of the afternoon with Seth, going through some simple drills on the spacious back lawn of Seth's gray stone mansion in the Cotton Wood Country Club. Troy's mom helped their efforts by playing receiver, running the routes Seth drew on his palm so Troy could practice his coverage. In the moments Seth let him stop to catch his breath, Troy couldn't help dreaming that one day he'd have his own stone mansion in Cotton Wood. He'd buy a place for his mom, too. He could just imagine the smile on her face when he handed her the keys.

"Not bad," Seth finally said, tucking the football they'd been using into a mesh bag filled with others, "but the biggest thing is going to be stopping the run."

Seth circled the large stone swimming pool and disappeared behind some bushes under the deck overlooking the pool and lawn. When he reappeared, he was dragging a huge blue tackling dummy.

"We gotta get you tackling low and hard and wrapping up with your arms," Seth said. "That's the key. It won't do us any good to get you to where the ball's going if you can't make the tackle."

"If Tate can do it," Troy said, getting into a ready stance on the lawn, "then I sure can."

"Hey," his mom said, "don't say that just because she's a girl."

"Yeah," Seth said, grunting with the dummy, "you'll get us all in trouble."

"I just mean she's pretty skinny," Troy said.

"It's not about size," Seth said, peeking out from behind the big blue bag. "You saw that today."

"I'll let you two bang around," Troy's mom said, wiping her brow. "I'm going to get a cold drink."

"Today it was about brains," Troy said, grinning at Seth as his mom walked away.

"But this will be about heart," Seth said, stepping aside after settling the dummy, whose sand-weighted base kept it upright, in the middle of the lawn. "Come on. I probably should have done this first, to see if the whole thing is worth even trying.

"Let's see what you've got."

Troy took a running start and unloaded on the dummy with all his might. Seth just shook his head. Troy hit it over and over, but Seth merely grunted and kept shaking his head.

Troy rubbed his shoulder and finally asked, "What?"

"You gotta hit it better than that," Seth said, "and wrap your arms around the dummy when you tackle. You hit like that and they'll run right through you like you're a wet paper bag."

Troy's stomach knotted tight. He felt his face go hot. He backed up and went at it again.

"Man," Seth said, still shaking his head.

"What?" Troy demanded, getting up and brushing off the grass.

"This ain't offense," Seth said. "You're on defense now. *Hit* the thing, will you?"

"I *am*," Troy said, fuming.

"Really hit it," Seth said, barking at Troy with the gruff edge to his voice he used when he coached the Tigers. "Not like some tap dancer. Come *on*. Get mad."

Being compared to a tap dancer made Troy see red. He coiled his body and launched himself at the dummy with all the fury he possessed.

CHAPTER SIXTEEN

"SO," TATE ASKED, "HE thinks you can play defense or he doesn't?"

Troy and Tate sat together, dangling their feet off the iron railroad bridge that crossed the Chattahoochee River not too far down the tracks from the back of Troy's house. A fat white moon glared down at them, its light buttering the slab-sided ripples in the water below. Above the river, black wings flickered, darted, and dove—bats searching for a meal.

"He said I got the basics down," Troy said, "and I finally made a tackle he liked."

"Sounds like he was pretty rough on you," Tate said.

"Well, he's our coach," Troy said. "I *want* him to treat me like everybody else."

"Why wouldn't he?" Tate asked.

Troy felt something boiling up inside him he couldn't really explain, an anger squeezed tight, making it fester. His hands gripped the cool, rusty metal girder above his head.

"You think they're going to get married?" he asked.

"I don't know, do you?" Tate asked quietly.

"They kiss each other a lot," Troy said, swatting at one of the few mosquitoes still alive this late in the fall. "But that's not it. It's the way they sometimes *look* at each other."

"That wouldn't be a bad thing, right?" Tate asked. "Seth Halloway for your dad? I mean, Seth marrying your mom."

Troy clenched his teeth and expelled hot blasts of air through his nose, shaking his head.

"You don't know what it's like," he said to her. "*Your* father is sitting on the couch with your mother right now watching a movie."

Tate put a hand on his leg. "You're right, I don't know, and I'm sorry, but Seth's a great guy. Look how he helped you get the job with the team."

"I'm helping him, too," Troy said. "I'm helping the whole team. My mom says ten thousand a game is a great deal for the Falcons, but as soon as it looks like someone might find out, I'm the one who has to go into hiding, like I'm doing something wrong. But I'm not. I've got a gift; that's what Gramp says it is. Why do adults always have to pretend? That's why you never know what they're really thinking."

Troy hopped up and started down the tracks for home. Tate scrambled after him.

"Don't get mad at *me*," Tate said, catching up to him and yanking on his arm to slow him down.

"I'm not," Troy said, his shoulders sagging. He put an arm around her shoulders and gave her a quick squeeze. "I'm sorry, Tate. You're the best friend anyone could want. I can't talk like this to anyone else. Heck, I shouldn't even be feeling like this. You're right. Seth is nice to my mom, to me, to our whole team. So why do I feel like this?"

Tate sighed and turned, starting down the tracks at an easy pace before she said, "The thing with your dad, not knowing him, not ever meeting him, I'm sure that makes it hard."

"My dad abandoned me," Troy said.

"But you don't want to abandon him," Tate said. "That's what I think this is. You really like Seth. Maybe you see him and your mom getting along and you can see Seth being a part of your family. That makes you happy on one side, but you kind of feel bad about it on the other side."

"The *stupid* side," Troy said, grabbing a stick from the edge of the bank and switching it back and forth between his hands.

"It's not stupid," Tate said. "It's just complicated. But

liking Seth doesn't have to mean anything bad about your father. If your father is anything like you, he'd want you to have Seth around."

They walked for a while, passing the spot where the path led up through the pine trees to Troy's house but not coming to a stop until they were even with the Pine Grove Apartments, where Tate lived.

"Okay," Troy said, patting her shoulder, "see you in the morning."

"You're sure it's okay that Nathan and I go with you?" Tate asked.

"My mom told me that Mr. Langan said he'd be happy to have you guys," Troy said.

"The owner's box," Tate said, staring into the glow of the streetlights scattered throughout the apartment complex. "Wow."

"I'd rather be on the field," Troy said. "I see it clearer down there. I don't know, I think it's something to do with being up close, little things like the way a quarterback licks his fingers if it's a pass, or how a running back will tighten his shoulder pads if he's getting the ball."

"But you've called the right plays from the stands before," Tate said. "You can do it. I know you can."

Tate started down the path and Troy stood there, watching her go.

"Tate," he said.

She stopped and turned.

"If that guy catches me tomorrow, I'm not running, and I'm not hiding anymore," Troy said.

"How's he gonna catch you?" Tate asked. "You'll be in the owner's box."

"I know," Troy said. "He probably won't, but if he does, it makes me feel better to know what I'm going to do."

Tate stood for a moment, then shrugged, letting her arms flop to her sides, and said, "I don't think that's a good idea."

"Probably not," Troy said, "but that's what I'm going to do."

CHAPTER SEVENTEEN

THE NEXT DAY, TROY, Tate, and Nathan rode to the Georgia Dome with Troy's mom and Seth. Troy couldn't help comparing the Tigers' upcoming championship game with the Falcons' position in their own league. A win today could put the Falcons in first place in their division, and they would begin to think realistically about a championship of their own. Before Seth left them for the team locker room, he pulled Troy aside.

"Hey," Seth said, "about yesterday."

"I know, you do what you have to," Troy said.

"Within limits, yes," Seth said, nodding his head. "But I got a little carried away yesterday. I'm sorry I pushed you so hard. Defense is different, you know. You've always been a quarterback, but I know you've got that mean streak under the surface, that thing you need to play defense. I was just trying to bring it out. I only want to help you, Troy. You know that, right?"

Troy looked up into the big player's eyes and saw real concern. Troy was afraid his own eyes might start to water, so he looked away and nodded and said, "Sure, I do. Thanks, Seth."

Seth mussed Troy's hair and they wished each other good luck. Troy's mom took Troy and his friends up the elevator and let the three of them off at the door of the Falcons owner's box before she hurried off to her job. Bob McDonough, Mr. Langan's security guard, a tall, silent former Secret Service agent, stood just inside the suite. When McDonough saw the three of them, he held out a hand and Troy, Tate, and Nathan all slapped him five on their way in. The sitting area was decked out in dark granite and wood, with couches, chairs, a bar, and a huge plasma TV screen. About a dozen adults dressed in blazers and pants or dresses milled about, along with a handful of kids, all eating, talking, or watching the pregame show on the big TV.

Nathan headed right for the buffet table, where he loaded a plate with four hot dogs, heaping them with mustard and sauerkraut and biting into one before he even sat down. Behind the bar, two servers dressed in white shirts and black pants busied themselves preparing food, pouring drinks, and refreshing the buffet. Kneeling on the floor with his back to the suite, a third server loaded bottles of soda into a refrigerator. Behind them, another door led into a kitchen with its own entrance for the workers out in the hall.

Mr. Langan appeared and shook hands with all of them, raising his eyebrows when his fingers came away from Nathan's mitt with a smear of mustard.

"Sorry," Nathan said through a mouthful of food.

"No, I'm . . . glad to see you kids eating," Mr. Langan said. "Get some sodas, too."

"I'm on that," Nathan said, hopping up from his spot on the couch, attacking the silver tub of iced drinks, and scooping up a handful of peanut butter cookies on the way back to his seat.

"Troy? Tate?" Mr. Langan said. "Hungry? There's more than just hot dogs."

Tate blushed and shook her head, and Troy said, "Thanks. I ate lunch before I came."

"Okay," Mr. Langan said to Troy, his face turning serious, "we win this one and Carolina loses and we're in first place. Just like that, last to first in four weeks. You feeling good?"

Troy gave him a thumbs-up.

"Great. Let me show you what we've got set up."

The suite was split into two separate sections connected to the lounge area. Nathan and Tate would sit in the bigger section of plush seats with Mr. Langan, his son Sam, who was the same age as they were, and the rest of the owner's family, business associates, and friends. Troy was shown through another door off to the side, a glassed-in area that looked like a small split-level office. Stairs led to the lower level, where three of the team's top executives sat at a long countertop covered with papers and telephones, looking down on the field.

Above them, in the darkest corner of the space, was a single desk with a high-backed leather chair that swiveled side to side.

"Right here," the owner said, pointing to the seat. "It's where I sometimes sit. You can use this headset to talk with the coaches."

Troy nodded, and Mr. Langan let himself out through the door, disappearing into the lounge. Troy sat down and put on the headset. He could see the entire field. In front of him was also a computer, a pair of binoculars, and a gray box with a control for the headset's volume and a mute button. Another plasma TV hung from the ceiling for watching replays. Troy wouldn't, though, because he'd need to look carefully for which players the Seahawks sent on and off the field.

While he couldn't exactly explain how he knew what the other team was going to do, he did know that different kinds of players meant certain formations and plays. Two tight ends and one wide receiver, for example, made it more likely a team would run the ball than if they had no tight ends and three wide receivers instead.

Troy heard the voice of Jim Mora, the Falcons'

defensive coordinator, on the other end of the headset.

"Troy? These guys are pretty darn good," Coach Mora said. "We're going to need you today. You all set, buddy? You ready to go?"

"Yeah," Troy said, locating the coach down on the sideline and returning his wave. "You?"

"One hundred percent," the coach said, giving a thumbs-up.

From where Troy sat, he couldn't see his friends or Mr. Langan on the other side of the partition. With the executives busy talking on their phones, taking notes, and conferring with each other in low tones, Troy felt completely isolated—a good thing. He turned the volume knob on the headset all the way down and let his eyes scan the field, floating over the space where the Seahawks sent players in and out from the sideline and huddled on the field. He needed to absorb the entirety of what the Seahawks did. It would take a couple of series—two or three, depending on how many plays they ran—before the patterns would emerge, just like the holograms on the comics page in the Sunday paper. When they did, Troy would see clearly what the Seahawks' next step would be. He'd know the play.

The first two times he'd done this, Jim Mora had pestered him, asking when it would happen. Then, two weeks ago, before their game against Tampa Bay, Troy explained that the best thing was to just let him be, and he was right. Tampa Bay had run just eight plays and hadn't even completed their second series when it hit him. He knew the coach wouldn't pester him today.

The Seahawks won the toss, received the kickoff, and drove down to the Falcons' seventeen-yard line on a ten-play drive before kicking a field goal on fourth and six. Troy watched, keeping his mind blank, just letting the information sink in, but for some reason—maybe because he was so far from the field—things seemed fuzzy, like talking on a cell phone with a weak signal. Seth shuffled off the field with the rest of the defense. Several times during the series, he'd been knocked flat by the Seahawks' offensive line. Twice he got to the hole a split second too late to make a tackle, and another time his pass drop was too shallow to keep the tight end from making a twenty-yard reception.

The Falcons took the ball, sputtering after just five plays, ten yards short of the fifty-yard line, and punted to the Seahawks. Three plays later, Shaun Alexander, the Seahawks' star runner, blasted through a hole up the middle. Seth threw himself in front of the runner, but Alexander lowered his shoulder and plowed right through Seth, all the way to the Falcons' forty-four before being brought down by DeAngelo Hall. Seth got up slowly, barely making it back to the defensive huddle, and was late calling the play that Coach Mora signaled in. The Seahawks snapped the ball and Matt Hasselbeck completed a touchdown pass to an uncovered receiver. The Georgia Dome erupted in boos.

Jim Mora didn't say anything, but Troy noticed him conferring with Seth as he came off the field and both of them looking up at the owner's box, obviously wondering if Troy's genius was close to kicking in. Troy swallowed and wondered if the whole thing with Peele, and worrying and watching the game from the owner's box, had stifled his gift. The Falcons' offense sputtered again, racking up only thirteen yards before fumbling and leaving the field under more boos. Two plays later, the Seahawks scored again on a thirty-seven-yard run by Alexander.

With the score now 17–0, one of the executives beneath Troy turned around holding up a red telephone and saying Troy's name until he came out of his trance.

"Troy," he said. "Mora is asking if something's wrong with your headset. He's talking to you and you're not answering."

"Oh," Troy said, "sorry. I've got the volume down. Thanks. I'll get with him."

Troy turned the volume up and heard Jim Mora's heavy breathing.

"You got anything?" Mora asked.

"I'm sorry, Coach," Troy said. "I'm trying."

"I know you said not to push you, buddy," the coach said, "but we're taking a beating down here. If we wait much longer, this thing might be too far gone to save. Is something wrong?"

Troy clenched his fists. His palms were slick with sweat. He shook his head to try to clear the cobwebs.

Just then one of the servers pushed into the small space carrying a tray of drinks.

Big pale eyes locked onto Troy from behind their thick round lenses. A small smile crept onto the face of Brent Peele.

"Troy," Coach Mora said, his voice urgent, "I said, 'Is anything wrong?'"

"Yeah," Troy said. "A lot."

CHAPTER EIGHTEEN

THE REPORTER WHIPPED OUT a miniature camera from underneath his tray, snapping a one-handed picture, the flash leaving a yellow spot in Troy's vision.

"I *knew* it was you," Peele said in a hushed whisper as he tucked the camera into his pants pocket. He wore the uniform shirt and tie of the other servers.

Troy removed his headset, shook his head, and said, "I'll talk to you, but not now."

"After the game?" Peele asked, pointing at him with the tray still balanced in his other hand.

"Yes," Troy said. "I promise."

"Okay, tell me this and I'll leave you alone until after the game," Peele said. "You're Troy White, right?"

Troy sighed and said, "Yes."

"Your mom's the PR assistant for the Falcons."

"If you know, why are you asking me?" Troy said, glaring.

"I *thought* I knew," Peele said with a mean smile growing on his face. "But I'm a reporter. I gotta confirm things."

"Good for you," Troy said. "Now, let me do this."

Troy angled his head toward the field, where the Falcons received the kickoff. Peele gave him a knowing nod, turned with his tray, and closed the door.

Troy took a deep breath and let it go, the anxiety of the day escaping his chest like air from a leaking balloon. He pulled the headset back on and returned his eyes to the field.

"I'm here," Troy said to Coach Mora.

"What happened?" Mora asked.

"Nothing," Troy said. "I'm fine. I think I'll have it next series."

Troy watched the Falcons complete a long pass that put them in field-goal range before they sputtered again. They tried the field goal but missed, turning the ball back over to the Seahawks.

As the Seattle offense took the field, Troy saw three receivers and the fullback jogging for the huddle. His gift kicked in.

He cupped his hand over the microphone, pulling it close to his mouth, and said, "Middle screen. Middle screen."

"You sure?" Mora asked.

"Pretty much," Troy said, and he watched the coach make a flurry of hand signals to Seth, who stood apart from the other defensive players. Seth turned and began shouting to his teammates. The Seahawks broke their huddle and jogged to the line of scrimmage. Hasselbeck looked the defense over and took the snap, dropping back as if to throw a pass. The Falcons' linemen broke through in a wave that reminded Troy of the Dunwoody Dragons.

Hasselbeck kept backpedaling, drawing the defenders toward him. The fullback suddenly spun around and held up his hands. Hasselbeck lofted the ball toward him. That's when, out of nowhere, Seth Halloway appeared, leaping in front of the fullback and snatching the pass.

The crowd howled and Seth hit the ground running. Hasselbeck came for him, but Seth gave his shoulders a twitch, faking one way, then running the other. The Seahawks' quarterback dove, arms flailing, and fell to the turf. Seth didn't stop until he reached the end zone. The Georgia Dome crowd went berserk

Although the Falcons' defense dominated the game from that point on, the offense couldn't seem to get its rhythm. The first half ended with Atlanta still down, 17–7. The executives below Troy conferred in whispers, checking their computers for statistics. The door beside Troy swung open. He half expected to see Peele, but Mr. Langan appeared, closed the door, and rested his hands on the desk in front of Troy.

"You had some trouble?" Mr. Langan asked.

"I couldn't see the patterns at the beginning," Troy said, hoping the owner wasn't referring to Peele. Troy wanted to focus on the game, not the reporter. If he won the game and put them into first place, it would make what he planned on doing with Peele more acceptable. As Seth always said, winning was the ultimate deodorant. It could turn even the smelliest situation into something sweet.

"You're on track now, though?" Mr. Langan asked.

"I am," Troy said.

The door opened behind Mr. Langan. A tray appeared with drinks and food, but it wasn't Peele carrying it. The female server squeezed past Mr. Langan, offering Troy a plate of hot dogs with a bag of chips and a large chocolate chip cookie. Troy took one of each, along with a bottle of water, before she served the men below.

Mr. Langan descended the small set of steps to talk with his executives, while Troy slathered ketchup on one of the dogs before taking a huge bite. The worry and excitement made him as hungry as Nathan. By the time he'd finished, Mr. Langan had gone and the team had begun to dribble back out into the bench area. Troy saw Jim Mora pick up his headset, so he put his own back on, stuffing a last bit of cookie into his mouth before answering the coach.

Troy saw the patterns after only a few plays, and the

Falcons' defense gave up barely a handful of yards. The Atlanta offense still struggled, though. Finally, late in the fourth quarter, the Falcons completed a long pass to Joe Horn, who lowered his shoulder, blasted through the free safety, then dashed into the end zone to make it 17–14.

With less than three minutes to go, Troy knew the Seahawks would just try to run out the clock. They wouldn't pass the ball because an incomplete pass would stop the clock. On first down, he predicted a sweep to the left. That's what Seattle did, and Seth stopped them for a two-yard gain. When Troy saw a second tight end jogging out onto the field and the fullback leaving, he smiled and his heart gave a leap.

"Coach," he said into his microphone, "call a time-out!"

"We only have one left," Mora said, "and Coach McFadden wants to save it for the offense."

"Coach! You have to! I need to talk to Seth!"

The executives below him in the box spun around at the sound of Troy yelling. His faced heated up and he cleared his throat.

"Please," he said, quieter now. "We can win this, but I have to talk to Seth."

"'Cause you know the play?" Mora said. "Just tell me."

"You don't have a defense for what Seth needs to do," Troy said. "I have to explain it to him."

"Troy, if we call a time-out, they could easily change the personnel, and the play you *think* they're going to run will change too," Mora said. "We'll waste the time-out for nothing."

"They won't," Troy said.

"If I call time-out and you're wrong," Mora said, growling, "I don't know if you'll get fired, but I sure will. Don't do this to me, Troy, unless you're absolutely certain."

Troy swallowed. Coach Mora was right. With the additional time to consider, Mike Holmgren, Seattle's head coach and an offensive wizard, could easily change his mind and use another play. Troy looked down at the executives scowling up at him, but he knew he was right.

"Do it, Coach. *Please.*"

Mora jumped out onto the field, signaling time-out to the referee. Seth jogged over to the sideline and Mora offered him his headset. Coach McFadden marched through the crowd of players and put a hand on Mora's shoulder, spinning him around and talking angrily. Troy shifted his attention to Seth, who removed his helmet, put the headset on over his sweat-plastered hair, and asked, "What's up, buddy?"

"They're going to run a counter trey to the weak side," Troy said.

"Troy, that's great," Seth said, "but why the time-out? Why didn't you just tell Mora that and have him signal it in? McFadden's about to blow a gasket."

"Because we need a turnover," Troy said, "or this thing's over. Shoot the strong-side A gap. If you follow the pulling guard, you might be able to hit the quarterback when he hands off the ball, hit him hard, and make him fumble. You can do it."

The referee blew his whistle, signaling the end of the time-out, and Troy heard the coaches shouting all around Seth.

"Did you hear me?" Troy said, raising his voice to a quiet scream.

"Yes," Seth said. "You're right. It might work."

"It *will* work," Troy said. "It has to. Go."

Seth handed the headset to Mora and ran back out onto the field, gesturing to his teammates and breaking the huddle so they could meet the Seahawks at the line. During the excitement, Troy hadn't kept an eye on the Seahawks, and as they came to the line, his stomach dropped.

CHAPTER NINETEEN

"TROY," MORA SAID INTO the headset.

"I know," Troy said. "I see."

The Seahawks had changed personnel during the time-out, exactly what Coach Mora had been afraid of.

"Will they still run it? They've got three wide receivers."

Troy wasn't sure, but he didn't want the coach to know that.

"Yes," Troy said. "They'll run it."

As Hasselbeck began his cadence, Seth eased up toward the line of scrimmage. Just before the snap, he darted at the offensive guard. The center hiked the ball. The guard pulled. Seth shot through the empty space a split second before it closed. The quarterback did a complete turn, extending the ball. The runner took a jab step to the strong side before cutting back toward the weak side, providing the delay Seth needed.

As the quarterback handed off the ball, Seth hit him from behind, crashing his arms down on the quarterback's hand, sending the ball scooting across the turf and the crowd into a frenzy. Demorrio Williams came from around the far side end, scooped up the fumble, broke a feeble tackle by Shaun Alexander, and raced toward the end zone. On his way there, Bobby Engram, the Seahawks' speedy wide receiver, closed the gap and grabbed hold of Demorrio's shoulder pad.

Demorrio spun, tumbling, and pitched the ball back to DeAngelo Hall. No one could catch him. When he got into the end zone, DeAngelo slid down on his knees and raised both arms up to the crowd. The noise washed over Troy, crashing from one side of the stadium to the other, with people waving their arms and banners and hats, so that Troy could only think of a movie he'd seen in science class about an enormous bee hive.

The executives jumped up, spilling their drinks, hooting, and clapping one another on the back. They pushed one another for the chance to bound up the steps and slap high-fives with Troy. Mr. Langan burst back through the door, too, slapping him a high-five, then hugging him tight. Tate and Nathan barged into the small space and hollered and danced around with Troy.

When the excitement died down and everyone collected their breath, Troy got back on the headset. His work wasn't done. The Falcons had to kick off to Seattle, and the Seahawks would get a final chance to score. But with only 1:43 left and Troy calling the plays to perfection, time soon ran out, and the Falcons won the game, 21–17.

Troy left his seat and entered the lounge area, where everyone stood chattering excitedly. The Carolina score came up on the TV screen, showing that they'd lost to New Orleans, putting the Falcons in first place. A cheer went up, and that's when Troy felt a hand on his shoulder.

"Now we talk, right?" Brent Peele said, nodding his head toward the bar and the entrance to the kitchen beyond it.

CHAPTER TWENTY

"OKAY," TROY SAID, TURNING to follow him.

Another hand grabbed Troy, from behind this time, spinning him back, and Tate said, "What are you doing?"

"That thing we talked about," Troy said, angling his head toward the reporter dressed as a server. "That's Peele."

"The waiter?"

"He just dressed like a waiter to get in here."

"Don't do it," Tate said, stamping her foot. "I'm telling you."

"I have to," Troy said. "I said I would."

"You don't have to keep your promise to that guy," Tate said.

Nathan stood next to her, nodding heartily. "My dad

says the only thing lower than a newspaper reporter is whale poop, but I don't blame you if you want to get into the papers. There's no such thing as bad publicity, right?"

Troy shook his head and said, "Anyway, I promised."

He shrugged Tate's hand off and followed Peele into the kitchen. The reporter removed a small tape recorder from his pocket and clicked it on so that a small red light glared at Troy like the eye of a snake. Peele offered him a box to sit on, then turned, closed the door, and threw home the deadbolt, locking them in.

"How did you know I was here?" Troy asked.

"*I'm* the reporter, kid," Peele said, holding up the recorder to prove his point. "It took me a couple days, asking around quietlike, but I found out about this new ball boy who was Tessa's son. She's new to the team. You're new. One plus one makes two. I figured they'd keep you hidden after I almost got you last week, and what better place to hide than the owner's box? I got my hands on the guest list and saw you there. A guy I know runs the catering in the dome. He put me on the kitchen staff, and here we are."

"Why did you follow us the other day to Seth's doctor?" Troy asked.

"Uh-uh," Peele said, shaking his head. "My turn now. Tell me how you do it."

Troy stared at him.

"Look, kid," Peele said like an old friend. "I know

you're not doing anything wrong. That's not what this is about, and it's not about Halloway, either. But people are going to find out. There's no way you can keep this thing secret forever. I just want to be the one who writes about it first, that's all. You might as well tell me. I'm a hometown guy. You don't think I want the Falcons to lose, do you? They're my team, too, you know. They win, we sell papers."

Troy took a deep breath and began to explain his gift and how his family called him a football genius. As Troy spoke, Peele's small mouth grew tighter and tighter. The white scar that ran from beneath his nose to the corner of his mouth began to do a little dance, tugging at the reporter's lip like a fishing line. Troy wanted to ask if Seth really gave it to him, but instead he finished by proudly recounting the story of the game they just played. He explained how he'd begged for a time-out, predicted the counter trey, and told Seth to attack it from the backside.

Peele inhaled sharply and said, "Let me get a couple things straight."

"Okay," Troy said, nodding eagerly, wanting to explain.

"You know what the other teams are going to do?"

"Yes."

"You know the plays they're going to run?"

"Yes. I see the patterns."

"Right," Peele said, "patterns. And you tell the

coaches so they can signal it in to Seth Halloway. He knows exactly what they're going to do, so not only can he change the defense, but he personally can get right to where the ball is going to be?"

"Yes."

"Because no way could Seth Halloway be playing like this without knowing the plays, right?"

"Well," Troy said, "Seth's a great player."

"Was. He *was* a great player," Peele said.

"And he still is," Troy said, scowling.

"With your help?" Peele said in a nice, appreciative way. "He's your friend, right?"

"Yes, I help Seth."

"And if you didn't give him the plays," Peele said, "how do you think he'd do? Look," Peele continued, dropping his voice to an even lower, more sympathetic volume. "This is a rough game. Seth's old. That's no sin. Honestly, though, he couldn't do this without you telling him the plays, could he?"

Troy looked down at his hands and said, "I guess not."

"I mean, the whole team wouldn't be making this playoff run, would it?" Peele asked.

"No," Troy said, getting excited about the great thing he'd done, "and Coach McFadden's job is on the line, so they have to win. He's such a great guy, you know?"

Peele nodded that he knew, then asked, "And you

started all this about the same time your mom got the job, isn't that right?"

"Yes, she got the job," Troy said. "Then she almost lost it, but I showed them what I can do."

"They were going to fire her?" Peele asked, raising his eyebrows in shock.

Troy nodded. "They actually did. It was this whole mix-up. I had a press pass, and I went out into the bench area and got thrown out. I was trying to help, and so was she."

"And when the Falcons figured out that you could help them get the other team's plays, they hired your mom, too?"

"Well, they were . . ."

Troy hesitated, a little confused and wanting to be clear.

"'Cause she technically wasn't working for the team anymore," Peele said. "Right?"

"Right."

"But once they found out what you could do, they weren't going to leave her out in the cold. Kind of a package deal, right?"

"Yes," Troy said, "it was a package deal, kind of, but my mom's great at what she does. It's a win-win."

"That's super," Peele said, grinning. "And Mr. Langan, he's got to be thrilled with all this."

"He is," Troy said, nodding and offering up a small

chuckle, thinking about those ten-thousand-dollar checks.

"Man, look at you," Peele said, shaking his head. "You're traveling around with the team and sitting in the owner's box. Wow."

Troy smiled back, shook his head, and said, "I told them you'd get it."

"Oh yeah," Peele said. "I get it. You get the plays and send them down on the coach's headset. It's a nice combination of human ingenuity and the latest technology."

"Yeah," Troy said.

"Would you say that's right?" Peele asked. "Can I quote you on that, the combination of ingenuity and technology?"

"That's what it is," Troy said, feeling like a weight had been lifted from his chest.

"But they didn't want you talking to me, though, right?" Peele asked.

"Well, they didn't know," Troy said.

"So, your mom, Mr. Langan, and Seth," Peele said, "they all wanted to keep this thing pretty quiet?"

"Sure," Troy said. "They'll probably kill me when they find out, but once they know you get it and that you're on our side, it'll all work out."

A sudden pounding on the other side of the door made Troy jump from his seat. The door handle rattled and shook, and someone began pounding again so hard that cracks of light appeared in the frame as the door bowed in.

"Troy!" Seth's voice boomed at him through the door. "It's me, Seth! Troy, are you in there? Open up!"

CHAPTER TWENTY-ONE

PEELE FUMBLED WITH HIS tape recorder, snapping it off and jamming it into his pocket. Troy reached for the deadbolt.

"No." Peele hissed, blocking Troy's hand and shaking his head from side to side. "Don't let him in."

"It's Seth," Troy said.

"He's an animal," Peele said. "Who knows what he'll do? Wait. Let me get out of here first."

Peele crossed the small kitchen and reached for the service door before he turned and said, "Give me a minute or who knows what he'll do."

"Well, don't write that about him," Troy said.

"I won't," Peele said. "That I won't write, but let me get away. I don't want any trouble right now. I've got a deadline for this thing."

Peele disappeared, and Troy winced at the loud pounding from the other side of the door.

Finally, he said, "Seth, stop it. I'm here. Everything's fine."

"Then open up," Seth said.

"Okay, but calm down," Troy said, sliding the bolt free.

Seth pushed inside, nearly knocking Troy over. The star linebacker was wearing his football pants and turf shoes with just a sleeveless, sweat-soaked undershirt so that his shoulders and arms bulged like cannonballs above fists clenched for fighting. The underside of his right forearm bore a bleeding welt where a nasty rub on the artificial turf had burned right through his outer layer of flesh. His hair, wet and stringy, spattered flecks of sweat across Troy's face as Seth whipped his head around, looking for Peele. Behind Seth, Tate and Nathan peered through the doorway into the kitchen.

"Where is he?" Seth growled. "That rat."

"Why did you guys do this?" Troy asked his friends.

"We took Mr. Langan's elevator down to the tunnel to get your mom," Tate said. "I went looking for her, but Nathan saw Seth coming out of the press conference room on his way into the locker room and . . ."

"It's a good thing they did," Seth said, banging a taped and bloodstained fist against one of the cabinets level with his head. "You might have talked to that guy."

"I . . . did talk to him," Troy said, softly.

Seth froze and stared down at him.

"It's okay, Seth," Troy said, smiling. "He wants the team to win, too. You think it does him any good if the team loses? We win and he sells papers."

"Is that what he said to you?" Seth asked in a quiet, furious voice, barely moving his lips.

"Well, it makes sense," Troy said, looking toward his friends now, eager for their support.

Nathan nodded and quietly muttered his agreement. Tate kept her lips sealed tight.

Seth shook his head, exhaled sharply, and said, "Well, what's done is done. Come on. You might as well all come back down with me and wait in the family lounge. There's no sense in Troy hiding up here anymore. He'll be famous in the morning."

Without explaining, Seth pushed past them, through the suite where the remaining guests were. They broke out into polite applause for the star linebacker. At the door, Nathan spun around and took a bow.

"Come on, hambone," Tate said, tugging him by the belt. "They're not cheering for you."

Seth took them down the private elevator and showed them the family lounge.

"You guys wait in there. I'll see your mom and tell her to meet you, and I'll get showered up."

Seth started to turn, but Troy put a hand on his arm.

Seth winced, snapping his arm away and shaking it.

"Sorry, Seth," Troy said, realizing that he had mistakenly touched the bloody turf burn.

"That's all right," Seth said, gritting his teeth. "I'll get it covered up with a bandage and it'll be a lot better."

"I mean, about Peele," Troy said. "It's just that I keep telling everyone that I'm not doing anything wrong, and I'm not."

Seth put one of his taped and bloody hands on Troy's shoulder and looked down at him sadly. "I know that's what you think, Troy. And I know you didn't mean anything, but tonight, we better go out and celebrate and have a real good time and enjoy the Falcons being in first place.

"I know you didn't mean it, but I think when you see what's in the newspaper tomorrow morning, this whole thing is going to come crashing down."

CHAPTER TWENTY-TWO

TROY LAY AWAKE WITH only the whisper of the pine boughs outside his window to keep him company. The moon, so bright the night before, could make itself seen only as a pale ghost through an occasional thin spot in the dark, rolling clouds. He wished his mother had yelled at him, stamped her foot, grounded him, something, anything but what she'd really done. Instead, after hearing everything that had happened, she'd only looked at her feet and shaken her head slowly back and forth. When they dropped Tate and Nathan off at their homes, his mother barely had enough breath to say goodnight. The rest of the evening, she sat in her chair with the TV off, sipping tea and staying quiet. When Troy tried to talk to her, she told him it was okay, but she looked at him in a sad and hopeless way that let him know it wasn't.

During a night of fitful half sleep, bad dreams, and lying awake, Troy's mind revolved around many different emotions: despair, frustration, fear, even anger. But when he woke for the final time and enough light seeped in through the curtains of his small bedroom so that he could call it morning, it was anger that prodded him free from the tangle of covers. Didn't his mom see? Why shouldn't he be famous? He'd take care of her when he was. He told her that. He wasn't like his father. Not at all. Didn't she believe that?

Troy yanked his clothes on and snatched his jean jacket from the front closet, then marched down the winding dirt track. Troy sniffed the air, smelling the red clay soil, the pines, and what he thought would be the coming rain. A black squirrel darted out into the path with a nut of some kind filling its mouth, flicked its tail, then darted back the other way, afraid of a twelve-year-old boy. His own heart began to race at the sight of the newspaper, lurking in its own bright blue plastic capsule beneath the mailbox.

Troy tugged it free and held his breath. He expected to have to dig two or three pages into the sports section to find whatever Peele had written. He didn't have to go that far.

On the front page, right beneath the paper's own

banner, standing three inches high in black ink, the headline cried out:

BAD BIRDS

A picture of Seth's snarling face behind his helmet's mask bore the caption *Falcons' Seth Halloway and owner John Langan conspired with PR assistant Tessa White to use a twelve-year-old boy—White's own son, Troy—to help steal opposing teams' plays for Atlanta's playoff run.*

Troy's legs turned to jelly. He staggered and stumbled on the lip of the dirt track, plopping down on his bottom in the long, damp grass.

With trembling fingers, Troy read through the article, which covered another ten inches of the front page before continuing on the inside. No one else had said anything to Peele. Mr. Langan, Seth, and his mother had all given the response of "No comment," and Mr. Langan referred the newspaper to his lawyers. Troy read all the way to the end in the futile hope that somewhere in the story, Peele would reveal the truth the way Troy had explained it.

Instead, the writer had twisted Troy's words to fit Peele's own theory that they were stealing their opponents' play calls by intercepting the radio signals between the coach's headset and the quarterback's helmet, or by using an uncanny ability to read lips, even though most coaches covered their mouths as they spoke into their headsets to call the plays. Peele even interviewed the head of research at a military contractor who said reading lips through a piece of paper was extremely easy with thermal imaging. That section was followed by Troy's own admission that they had used "a combination of ingenuity and technology."

Troy didn't know how long he sat there. Several cars whooshed past on the rural highway, kicking up small clouds of grit and dust that floated down on Troy like nightmare snow. When he heard crackling sticks in the nearby pine trees, he looked up and saw Tate, breaking one last branch to gain entrance to the dirt driveway.

"I saw you," she said in a harsh, accusing tone. "I saw you from the path in the woods, sitting up here, hiding in the grass."

"I wasn't hiding, Tate," Troy said, his voice sounding weak and pitiful as she brandished a rolled-up morning paper.

"I'd hide if I were you," Tate said, waving the paper even higher. "I can't believe you did it. After everything Seth's done for you? Coaching you? Believing in you? How could you?"

Tate snapped open her paper and read, "'Troy White readily admitted that Seth Halloway's recent incredible performances couldn't have happened without the specific knowledge of the plays that opposing teams were about to run.'"

Tate slapped the paper down at her side and asked, "How could you do that to him?"

"I didn't," Troy said. "I didn't mean to. Peele lied about everything. He's making it sound so bad, but all I wanted to do was tell the truth. We're not doing anything wrong. It's a gift. You called it that. Why do I have to hide it? It's all lies."

"That's why you had to hide it," Tate said, raising her voice to a shout. "Everyone told you this would happen, but you didn't listen. You think Seth's going to coach us now, after this? You wanted people to know. You wanted to be in the paper. Well, now you're in the paper, and so is everyone else, and you've *ruined* everything."

Tate wadded up the paper and threw it at him and ran off down the dirt track, turning into the trees and disappearing toward the Pine Grove Apartments.

Troy just sat there, listening to the sound of his own breathing and wanting to wake up and have it all be a dream. His chest ached, he wanted it so bad. When he heard the sound of his mom's VW Bug chugging up the dirt path, he looked at the pale green car with a dull face. He hadn't moved from the grass.

The Bug stopped and his mom reached across the passenger seat and rolled down the window.

"Get in," she said, her voice as flat and lifeless as a pancake without syrup.

Troy stood and stepped toward the car.

"Bring that paper," she said without looking at him,

her hands clasped to the steering wheel.

Troy looked back at it, lying there in the tall grass next to Tate's crumpled version.

"I don't want you to read it, Mom," he said. "Please."

"I already heard what's in it," his mom said. "Bring it. I need to see it all before our meeting."

Troy picked it up off the grass and asked, "Who are we meeting?"

CHAPTER TWENTY-THREE

"PLEASE GET IN," TROY'S mom said with an edge in her voice that he wasn't used to.

Troy climbed in, set the newspaper down between them, and buckled his seat belt. His mom threw the car into gear and they jumped forward, swerving out onto the country road.

"You gonna tell me where we're going?" Troy asked.

"Mr. Langan wants to see us," his mom said.

"What about school?" Troy asked.

"You'll be a little late," his mom said.

As they approached the main highway, the old peanut man looked up from his pot on the side of the road and waved. Troy's mom glanced at her watch, then put on her blinker and turned into the dirt spot on the side of the road.

"What about Mr. Langan?" Troy asked

Troy's mom said nothing and rolled down her window.

"How's my beauty today?" the old-timer asked in a thick southern drawl.

"Today's not a great one," she said, "but I'll take some peanuts."

"'Course you will," the old man said.

He tottered over to the black pot that hung over a wood fire behind his ancient pickup truck. Carefully, he ladled a portion of boiled peanuts into a cone of newspaper. When he returned, he deftly seized Tessa's two dollars, the bills disappearing into the front of his overalls like magic as he handed her the peanuts.

"Thing about newspapers these days," he said, nodding at the paper cone, "ain't really good for much other'n boiled peanuts or maybe if'n you got a puppy you aim to house train."

A smile tugged at the corners of Tessa's lips as she thanked the old-timer and pulled away.

Troy didn't let her smile fade completely before he said, "Mom, I'm sorry. I didn't say that stuff. I mean, I didn't say it like that."

His mom bit into her lower lip, keeping her eyes on the road, and said, "Everyone told you not to talk to him, Troy."

"Everyone said he was trying to hurt the team," Troy said, "but that's not what he said. He made it like he wanted to help, like the best way to handle it was to get it out, the truth."

"But that's not what came out, is it?" his mom said bitterly. "I mean, you don't really think that's the reason the Falcons hired me, do you?"

"Mom, you know I don't," Troy said. "You had the job before any of this. I just said that I got you fired by my screwing up and then they rehired you after they saw what I could do."

"Or that we'd 'kill you' if you didn't help steal the plays?" she said, throwing a nasty glance his way that cut him to the bone.

"I didn't mean it like that," Troy said, hanging his head. "I just said it, you know, like an expression."

They pulled up to a red light, and his mom closed her eyes for a moment before exhaling through her nose and nodding her head. "I know you didn't mean it, Troy, but unfortunately, I don't think it matters what you meant. The damage is done."

"What did Mr. Langan say?" Troy asked.

"I didn't even speak to him," his mom said. "I just got a call from his assistant, who said you and Seth and I need to be in his office as soon as possible."

"Seth, too?"

She nodded and said, "He's the one who told me what the article said. He's already there with a bunch of the other players, getting their lifting and treatment done early."

When they pulled into Flowery Branch, the Falcons facility, Troy couldn't bring himself to look at the guard, but the man's voice sounded strained, as though he, too, knew what Troy had done. Troy's mom pulled into the employee lot. The two of them got out and circled around to the front of the building, where they went in the main entrance and up the carpeted stairs to the team's executive offices. Seth sat in the board room, looking out of place, dressed in workout gear as if he'd come right from the weight room. Across from him at the big mahogany table were Mr. Langan and Cecilia Fetters, all of them waiting for Troy and his mom.

They sat down next to Seth and across from Cecilia Fetters, his mom's boss. Mr. Langan sat at the head of the table in a dark suit with a crisp white shirt and a tie, his chin propped up on a steeple of fingers and his eyes red and moist around the edges.

"Thank you for coming in so early, Tessa," the owner said to Troy's mom. "As you know, we've got a serious problem. I've been up all night talking with the lawyers and the commissioner. I knew from the nature of the call I got from Peele last night that it was going to be bad."

Mr. Langan raised the newspaper before letting it drop back down onto the conference table and said, "I just didn't know it would be this bad."

CHAPTER TWENTY-FOUR

TROY STUFFED HIS HANDS, now sweaty and cold, beneath his legs. His face burned with shame; his clothes felt suddenly too tight.

"I'm so sorry, Mr. Langan," Troy's mom said in a small voice.

Cecilia Fetters snorted and shook her head as if she'd known all along things would end this way. Mr. Langan cleared his throat and turned his attention to Troy.

"Troy, I hope you don't really think we threatened you in any way to help the team," the owner said.

Troy dropped his eyes and shook his head.

Mr. Langan sighed and said, "I know how reporters can sometimes twist things around. It was one of the first things I learned when I bought this team, and I had to learn it the hard way, too."

"I'm sorry I talked to him," Troy said, looking up into the owner's sagging eyes and trying to keep his own eyes from flooding with tears. "I know I shouldn't have, but I thought he was on our side."

"And I thought the dome caterer would never let someone like Peele sneak around posing as part of the staff," the owner said, laying his hands flat on the table, "but we can't change what's already happened, neither of us, and we've got to play with the cards we've been dealt. I just wanted to make sure, from your own mouth, that you know we wanted this whole thing to be positive and that the only reason we tried to keep it quiet was because it's very difficult to explain to people and make them understand how you do what you do."

"I know," Troy said.

"Good," Mr. Langan said softly. "Now, as I'm sure you can imagine, we'll have to suspend your role with the team until this whole thing gets sorted out with the league. The commissioner is launching a full investigation, and right now it looks like we'll end up in federal court."

The words echoed through Troy's mind; he had the image of sitting in a witness box in his church clothes being questioned by angry lawyers.

"I'm sorry it turned out this way," the owner said, frowning and shaking his head. "Believe me, I'm going to do everything I can to get this resolved. I do agree with you, Troy, that neither you nor we have done anything wrong. We didn't steal anyone's signals or use anything other than your own God-given talents. Still, I have to be honest, the league isn't apt to see things that way. It's not like you're a player. If you were, they couldn't say anything about it. But being a twelve-year-old kid makes you stick out in a way that I'm pretty sure will allow them to figure a way to keep you out of the game.

"Now, if you wouldn't mind waiting with Seth downstairs, I think what Cecilia and I have to say to your mom will be a little easier."

When Seth rose from the table, Troy saw that he was wearing shorts and both his knees had bags of ice wrapped tightly to them with Ace bandages. Seth hobbled toward the door, though, obviously used to the pain and the ice treatment his knees required before and after almost every game.

"What are they saying to her?" Troy asked as he followed Seth down the back stairs, the clack of their feet loud and rhythmic on the metal steps.

"Nothing good," Seth said. "Come on with me. I'm going to change and then we'll meet your mom."

Seth banged open a door, leading Troy into the locker room, where several rows of huge lockers stood bursting with the players' equipment. At the end of each row stood a garbage can for spent ankle tape, used tissues, spit cups full of tobacco juice, and half-eaten food. The square cans, lined with thick gray trash bags, were big enough for Troy to sit down in. He sniffed. While the freshly painted metal lockers and the crisp red carpet made the enormous room look spotless, the hint of sweaty leather and workout clothes and garbage from the bins still drifted through the air.

Several other players sat or stood at their own lockers, fussing with their equipment, changing into workout clothes. Troy looked up at the rounded shadowy reflection of his own face in the black helmet that hung from a hook outside Seth's closet-sized locker. He reached up and traced a finger along the white-edged wing of the Falcons decal and bit his lip to keep his eyes from spilling tears.

Seth unwrapped his knees and let the bags of ice fall to the carpet. The skin surrounding the swollen knees was an angry red, almost like a sunburn. Seth dropped his gym shorts and tugged on a pair of jeans, then stripped off his shirt, stuffing it into a laundry bag before he stood up straight and threw the bag into the back of his locker.

Suddenly a low growling noise bubbled up out of his chest. Troy followed Seth's glare to the end of the row of stools, where Brent Peele leaned up against a locker with his tape recorder extended toward the seated form of John Abraham.

CHAPTER TWENTY-FIVE

THE MUSCLES RIPPLED IN Seth's neck and naked back. He threw his scarred shoulders back, marching toward Peele on bare feet, his limp gone. When Seth closed the distance to just a few lockers, Peele looked up. The reporter's face went red and the scar above his lip began to twitch, but he smiled big, exposing his sharp white teeth.

"Hello, Seth," Peele said, straightening up, his voice laced with a nervousness that didn't match his bold grin.

"Attacking me? I get that," Seth said. "You thought you were ready for the big leagues and I knocked you out, cold. The very fact that you never understood that's part of the game is the same reason why you never would have made it, no matter what I did to you. So, I get why you hate me, even though you have no right. But Tessa?

She never did anything to you, and you pulled her and an innocent kid into the mud."

"The kid might be innocent," Peele said, still sneering, "but the mom is as bad as you. Both of you, you don't care about this kid. You're using him to save your career. She's using him, too. Probably for money. Some mom. Gee, I wonder why the dad took off."

"You're trash," Seth said, and without pause he spun the reporter around, gripped him by the back of his belt and shirt collar, lifting Peele up nearly over his head before dumping him down, headfirst, into the enormous waste bin.

Peele shrieked, kicking his feet and scrabbling in the garbage to right himself. Seth marched back to his locker, pulled on his shirt, and sat down on the stool to lace up his sneakers as if nothing had happened. Only his mouth showed a grim, flat line of satisfaction.

Peele gained his feet inside the trash can and pulled a snotty tissue free from his collar. Spit stains, as brown as bug vomit, coursed down his white polo shirt, and the smear of a half-eaten breakfast burrito ran down the front leg of his jeans.

Peele gagged at the sight of the slimy green tissue, pitched it down on the carpet, and stabbed a long, bony finger at Seth, shouting the length of the locker room. "You think you can do this to me?"

Troy thought he heard John Abraham say "He just did" as the big defensive end, his eyes slits of glee, stepped gingerly around the reporter and headed toward the weight room.

Seth tugged his laces tight, got up, turned his back on the reporter, and said to Troy, “Let’s go.”

“You’re finished!” Peele screamed from behind them. “I’ll ruin you!”

When Seth slammed the locker room door closed behind them, Peele was still screaming, shouting obscenities and promising Seth that his days in the NFL were now over.

Troy looked up at Seth in the relative silence of the hallway, smiled, and said, “He can’t do anything to you, can he?”

Seth took a deep breath and let it out. He slowed his pace, and his limp returned. He looked down at Troy and said, “Honestly? I probably shouldn’t have done that.”

“But he can’t really ruin your *career*,” Troy said.

“Yes,” Seth said, putting his hand on the door that led to the parking lot and pushing it open, “he probably can. But let’s not talk about it. There’s your mom.”

Troy’s mom stood leaning back against her VW Bug, staring up at the empty sky as if she were watching a blimp cruise circles above the training complex. Troy walked briskly toward her, keeping pace with Seth until they came to a stop in front of her. She let her eyes drop from the sky, past them, and down to the ground.

“Mom?” Troy said hesitantly. “What happened?”

CHAPTER TWENTY-SIX

"MR. LANGAN WAS VERY nice," Troy's mom said in a voice sad and low enough to let them know that while the owner might have been nice, the result of her meeting was nothing good.

"But what happened?" Seth asked, gently touching a bent finger under her chin and raising it to look into her eyes.

Troy's mom shrugged. "Well, I always wanted to do some oil painting. Now I'll have the chance."

"He fired you?" Troy asked.

"No," his mom said, shaking her head, "not fired. I'm on leave . . . with pay, so that's the good news."

"But you didn't do *anything*," Troy said, his voice pitched with anger.

His mom smiled weakly and said, "Yeah, but we're a

package deal, remember? At least that's how it looks."

"Who cares how it looks?" Troy said.

"Every NFL team and every NFL team owner," Seth said. "That's the business."

"And they're asking me to keep a lid on things," his mom said.

"What's that mean?" Seth asked.

"No interviews. They're already starting to get calls from the national media," his mom said. "CNN, *Fox and Friends*, *Good Morning America*. Cecilia doesn't want me contributing to the 'circuslike atmosphere' she thinks is going to evolve."

"Circus?" Seth said. "The whole NFL is a circus. I remember watching the Falcons when I was Troy's age, with Deion Sanders, Jerry Glanville as the coach wearing his black hat, MC Hammer and Kris Kristofferson on the sidelines? *That* was a circus." He swatted the air and continued, "Cecilia Fetters has been looking for a way to bring you down ever since Mr. Langan made her hire you back. That's all this is."

Troy clenched his fists and looked back at the Flowery Branch facility. Without thinking, he said to Seth, "Peele's *lucky* you only dumped him in the trash. You should have bashed his—"

The look Seth flashed at him came too late. Troy bit down hard on his lower lip and clamped his mouth shut.

"Trash?" Troy's mom asked.

Seth took a deep breath and let it out slow, waffling his lips.

"Seth, I'm sor—"

Seth held up his hand. "It doesn't matter. She would have found out sooner or later."

"Found out what?" Troy's mom asked.

Seth told her what he had done.

"Oh no," his mom said. "*Why*?"

"Look," Seth said, "I can take the kind of junk he's written about me; that's part of the game. Smearing you? That's *not* part of the game. If he's gonna play rough like that, then he's gonna get roughed up a little himself."

"You just can't do that to the reporter of a big newspaper," Troy's mom said.

"Yeah," Seth said, "well . . . I just did. Let him rip me. Let them cut me. I'm almost at the end now, anyway. It's the NFL motto: Not For Long."

"You're not at the end. You're going to go to the Pro Bowl," Troy said.

"Not if I'm not on an NFL team," Seth said, laughing bitterly.

"If they're dumb enough to cut you," Troy said, "you'll get picked up by another team in a heartbeat."

Seth's face sagged and his voice went soft. "I'm old, buddy. These knees are about as bad as it gets. I'm old and I'm beat up, and, you know, honestly? I'm tired. You calling the plays for me lets me play the way I used to, the interceptions, getting to the line at the same time as the runner, busting up the middle and sacking the quarterback. Honestly? I don't want to go back to playing old and beat up and tired, and I don't think anyone is going to line up to sign me to, either. This just might be the end."

"It can't be," Troy said.

"Hey," Seth said, "you know what? Let's not even worry about it. Let's get you to school, and me and your mom will take some time off, go to the museum to get some ideas for her painting, and I'll work on our game plan against Valdosta and then we'll meet later at practice. We still got that."

Troy remembered Tate's harsh words and her dire prediction that Seth would no longer help them.

"You mean, you'll coach us?" Troy asked. "After I made this mess?"

"Hey, it's the state championship," Seth said, putting an arm around Troy's mom and giving her a smile and a quick hug. "Not a bad way for me to start my next career. I always wanted to get into coaching."

Seth's cell phone rang. He fished it out of his pocket, checked the number, and looked at Troy's mom. "That didn't take long."

"Who is it?" she asked.

Seth didn't answer her. He snapped open the phone and said, "Hello? Yes . . . Yes, I did . . . All right. I'll be right there."

Seth closed the phone and stuffed it back into his pocket.

"On second thought," Seth said to Troy's mom, "why don't you take Troy to school and I'll just meet you later on, maybe for lunch."

"Who was it?"

"Coach McFadden," Seth said. "He and Mr. Langan want to see me in his office. Now."

CHAPTER TWENTY-SEVEN

TROY WENT INTO THE school office and signed in late. The third-period bell rang, and he ran through the busy hallways toward Tate's locker. He found her slamming it shut and turning with her books toward Nathan, who was waiting to walk with her to science class.

"Hey," Troy said, grabbing her arm and spinning her around.

Tate scowled at him, as did Nathan.

"It's okay," Troy said, out of breath. "Seth's still coaching the team. He's mad, but mad at Peele, not me."

Tate's angry look melted. "He is?"

"What about that nasty article and all that crap you said?" Nathan asked.

"Seth understands," Troy said, frowning. "I didn't

say that stuff like that. Peele twisted it around. Seth knows."

"Cool," Nathan said. "Valdosta, watch out. You're looking at the next state champs!"

They all grinned and slapped high-fives.

Rusty Howell walked up and heard the good news, then asked, "Is our championship game really gonna be on TV?"

Troy nodded.

"Sweet," Rusty said, the freckles on his face glowing. "I'm going to get my dad to tape it. I hope they'll have replays. You connecting with me in the end zone for the state title? I can't wait."

"Sheesh, I gotta get a trim," Nathan said, running a hand over his bristles. "Who knows? Somebody from the Disney Channel sitting there, watching this game, they see me and next thing you know I'm on TV datin' Hannah Montana."

The bell rang, and Tate and Nathan hurried off. Troy dashed to his own locker for his books before arriving late to science class. In the hallways between classes, it seemed that every other person stopped to talk to him about the newspaper article. For those who didn't actually read the paper, word had spread through the school like wildfire, spawning rumors of Troy going to jail for his involvement in the scandal.

The crazy talk would have been enough to occupy

his mind, freeing him from the usual boredom of math vectors, the Boer War, plant cell structures, and Shakespeare's plays—which his teacher claimed were written in English. But what mostly kept Troy busy was the thought of the championship against Valdosta. By the end of the day, he'd filled his notebook with diagrams of pass patterns and defensive coverages he planned to discuss with Seth.

If the Tigers could win that game and Troy could become a championship quarterback, he knew everyone would forget about the nasty newspaper article. Also, if he couldn't use his football genius now, for the Falcons, Troy knew the other way to use it would be when he played in the NFL himself. Winning a state championship as the quarterback for the Duluth Tigers would put him well on his way to achieving that goal.

Everyone knew that the best high schools—football powerhouses like Norcross and Parkview and Valdosta's own varsity team—would recruit players from the junior league state championship game. If Troy could get a place on a team like that, then the path to playing at a Division I college and, ultimately, in the NFL would be a lot clearer.

The only downer during the day was when Jamie Renfro came up behind Troy at lunchtime.

"What kind of genius would say so many stupid things to a reporter?" Renfro asked his friends in a voice loud enough so Troy and his friends could hear them.

Troy clenched his fists, but Tate put her hand on his arm and said, "Don't go for the bait. He'd love nothing more than to get you into trouble so you can't play Saturday."

Troy nodded and bit into his sandwich, chewing mechanically.

On the way home from school, Nathan and Tate rode the bus past the Pine Grove Apartments and got off with Troy at the end of the drive that wound back through the pines to his house. Seth's yellow H2 sat snuggled up next to the VW Bug on the red dirt patch out front. On the porch, Troy's mom stood behind an easel alternately looking up at the pine trees and dabbing paint onto her canvas.

"They say to paint what you know," she said, wiping at a smear of paint on her nose with the back of her wrist, "and I see pine trees in my sleep."

Inside, Seth sat at the kitchen table hunched over his notebook and a stack of papers, drawing and writing furiously.

Troy took three sodas from the fridge and passed them out. Nathan grabbed a banana from the bowl on the table and began peeling it.

"Hey," Seth said, looking up when he finally realized the three of them were surrounding him at the table.

"I got some plays and coverages to show you," Troy said, holding up his notebook.

"Okay," Seth said, "but Troy, can I talk to you first?"

"Sure," Troy said.

"Outside?"

Troy shrugged at his friends and followed Seth out the back door. Seth took a few steps across the carpet of fallen pine needles and turned.

"You said a lot of things that Peele took out of context," Seth said, "things he twisted around so they would sound worse than you meant them."

"Yeah," Troy said, studying Seth's face.

"I just need to know, Troy," Seth said. "Did you talk to Peele about Doc Gumble and that vitamin shot I told you I was getting?"

"What?" Troy said, narrowing his eyes and shaking his head. "No. I didn't."

"And you're sure?" Seth asked.

"Yes," Troy said. "The only thing I did was ask him why he followed us that day."

"Followed us?" Seth said.

Troy bit into his lower lip and nodded. "I didn't say anything because, I don't know, it seemed so weird, I wasn't sure it was really him. I thought he took a picture of me and drove off. Why?"

Seth frowned and said, "That's what McFadden and Mr. Langan wanted to see me about today. They got word that Peele may be doing a story about me supposedly using steroids."

"But you're not," Troy said, the words coming out almost like a question.

Seth looked at him hard and said, "No. I'm not, and I never did. If you didn't say anything about that vitamin shot, something he could twist around, then I'm not worried. Peele might just be spreading a rumor. Come on, let's get back inside. Forget I even asked."

Together they returned to the kitchen. Troy flipped through his notebook, pointing out his ideas to Seth.

"I like it," Seth said. "We can combine your ideas with mine. I've been busy, too."

Seth held up the stack of papers he'd been working on when they arrived and said, "Take a look at this. I spoke to a newspaper reporter I know from down in Macon who gave me a heck of a scouting report on Valdosta. They run the Tampa Two defense, so I was thinking—"

"Wait," Troy said, holding up a hand. "A reporter?"

"Well, yeah, a guy I know," Seth said, tapping his pen on the notebook. "So I was thinking that maybe we'll play Rusty Howell in the slot, to really attack the seam up the middle of the field. We can—"

"Seth," Troy said, "I thought we hate reporters."

Seth looked up from his plan. "No. Peele's not our favorite person, but you can't hate a whole group of people. That's ignorant. There are good reporters just like there are good . . . I don't know, lawyers, doctors, agents, football players, prison guards. There's good and bad in any group of people. They're not all bad. My guy's even going to FedEx me some game film."

"Oh," Troy said, letting the revelation sink in before

pointing to the diagram of Rusty Howell against the Tampa Two. “So you’ve got the whole plan done already?”

“Ready for you to look at,” Seth said, grinning. “I’m smart enough to know I’m not that smart. You think I’m not going to get my football genius to look this over before I say it’s done?”

Troy felt his cheeks grow warm.

“And, you probably want to get some input from a lineman on all this stuff,” Nathan said, stepping in and planting a thick finger in the middle of the diagram and smearing it with banana grease. “Come on. Sheesh. That’s where you win these championship things, right at the line of scrimmage.”

Seth laughed, nodded his head, and said, “A lot of people might agree with that.”

“Hey, a lot of people might agree that the difference between winning and losing is a good kicking game,” Tate said, snapping her fingers at them repeatedly.

“How about a good coach?” Troy said. “Nothing’s more important than that.”

They all nodded and then listened as Seth explained how he figured his plan could beat Valdosta’s defense.

“And we haven’t even talked about our defense,” Seth said, turning to the last few pages of his notebook. “Because I think it’s going to be simple. Troy, did you tell these guys?”

CHAPTER TWENTY-EIGHT

"TELL US WHAT?" NATHAN said, pulling a bag of chips from the cupboard and digging in. "Sheesh, I'm the last to know everything."

"You know how Troy can predict what the other teams' offenses are going to do against the Falcons' defense? Seeing the patterns and all that?" Seth said. "So I figure, why can't we do that against Valdosta?"

"Who you gonna signal stuff in to?" Tate asked.

"Well, my mind-reading powers are on the fritz, so that's out," Nathan said, crunching on some chips.

"We don't need signals," Seth said. "Troy's going to be out there."

Nathan hooted at the idea, sending a spray of crumbs across the table.

"On defense?" Tate asked, brushing flecks of potato

chips off her shirt. "He's the quarterback. I thought you gotta protect the quarterback."

"There's no sense in protecting me. This is the state championship," Troy said, "maybe the only one we'll ever play in. It's on TV. Everyone will be watching. Half of Atlanta will be there under the lights at Georgia Tech's stadium. This is huge."

"And honestly," Seth said, wagging his head toward Nathan, "no offense to any of you guys, but if we can't do better on defense than we did against Dunwoody, we aren't going to be champs. We'll be chumps."

Troy explained how Seth had given him a crash course on playing defensive back, and then together they all listened as Seth leafed through his notebook, explaining his plan against Valdosta's offense. After a time, Troy's mom came in and swapped her paint things for the pots and pans she needed to whip up a meal of chicken rigatoni that they could all eat before heading off to practice.

After an early dinner, Seth drove Nathan and Tate to their homes so they could quickly change into practice gear. As they drove toward the school, the setting sun blinded them, the shadows grew long, and an autumn chill crept into the air.

When they pulled into the parking lot beside the practice field and Troy saw the silver car, he quickly rolled down the window, thinking he might be sick.

Seth cranked the wheel around, backed into a spot,

and asked, “What the heck are they doing here?”

“Who?” Nathan said, spinning around in his seat and craning his neck.

“Them,” Tate said, pointing before she let out a groan.

CHAPTER TWENTY-NINE

THE GRASS ON THE Tigers' practice field—like all but the most carefully manicured fields in the best stadiums—had withered during the thirsty autumn into a wiry brown carpet. Troy got out and slung his helmet under one arm, bounding every third step to keep up with Seth's steady, painful march across the field. Nathan and Tate jogged behind. Out beneath the faded goal-posts, standing in an odd cluster beside the ring of football players waiting on one knee, stood several adults, including Brent Peele, a uniformed Gwinnett County sheriff, and the fathers who assisted Seth, along with Mr. Renfro and his son, Jamie.

"Can I help you people?" Seth asked, his eyes protected from the falling sun by a pair of sunglasses.

Peele—whose cigarette Troy had smelled the moment

they got out of Seth's truck—exhaled smoke through his nose and chuckled, winning grins from Jamie Renfro and his father. A red-faced man Troy didn't recognize stepped forward and extended a hand for Seth to shake. He had combed-over hair and the tailored suit and crisp white shirt of a banker.

"Seth, I'm Jerry Flee, Flee with two e's," the man said, retracting his hand after Seth gave it a quick glance. "I'm the Duluth Junior Football League president. I'm sorry, Seth, you've done an amazing job and we can't thank you enough for taking over and getting the kids through the playoffs."

"We've still got a big game to play," Seth said, grinding his teeth.

"Well, that's what we came to talk to you about," Flee said, "and we're very sorry—the league, that is."

"The league," Seth said.

"Yes, we are," Flee said, nodding vigorously.

"And you would be?" Seth asked the cop.

The sheriff—really just a big fat blond kid fresh out of high school—cleared his throat and shifted nervously from one foot to the other, touching the gun in his holster but then flicking his fingers away as if it were red-hot.

"Officer Cussing," the cop said. "Just here to keep the peace, Mr. Halloway."

"What peace?" Seth said, looking around at the group of players assembled behind him. "Some trouble with these kids or something?"

"Trouble a loudmouth jerk like you is famous for," said Mr. Renfro, folding his thick arms across his chest and resting them atop the shelf of his ample beer gut as if he hadn't a care in the world.

The muscles in Seth's jaw rippled and his hands curled into concrete fists.

"Famous, huh?" Seth said.

Mr. Renfro nodded.

"And what would *you* be famous for?" Seth growled.

While Mr. Renfro snorted and mumbled, Flee produced several folded sheets of paper from the inside pocket of his suit coat and handed them to Seth with a now-trembling hand.

"If I could just point out to you, Mr. Halloway," Flee said in a quavering voice, "section 6, paragraph C, I think you'll understand completely what the league's position is on all this and why we really do have to go along with it."

"Along with *what*?" Seth asked, snatching the papers from Flee and searching through them.

"Why, Mr. Halloway," Flee said, blinking, "I'm very sorry. I thought you knew. You're being removed as coach of the Duluth Tigers."

CHAPTER THIRTY

"WHAT DO YOU MEAN 'removed'?" Troy asked, clutching the mask of his helmet so hard he could feel the rubber-coated metal against his finger bones.

"He can't coach the team," Peele said with a nasty smile. "He broke the rules."

"What rules?" Troy asked. "Seth didn't break any rules."

Seth looked up from the papers and rattled them in the air. "This says 'endangering the moral welfare of the players.' You underlined 'notorious use of controlled substances.' That's not me."

"*What?*" Troy said, his voice unbelieving.

"You can't just have any clown off the street coaching kids," Jamie Renfro said, sticking his chin out at Troy.

"He's an *NFL* player," Tate said, marching right up

to Jamie and sticking her face into his.

Jamie gave her a disgusted look, waved his hand like she didn't matter, and said, "We'll see for how long."

"While the league certainly appreciates the fine effort," Flee said with a frown, "with the facts Mr. Peele and Mr. Renfro have brought to light—facts that will be known and 'notorious' after everyone reads tomorrow's newspaper—we can't allow you to coach the team."

"I volunteered to do this," Seth said, curling his upper lip.

"And it's very kind," Flee said, "but the rules are what they are. I'm not saying what's true and what isn't, but the allegations alone mean we have to suspend you from coaching the team."

"And if you're wrong about these allegations?" Seth said. "Which you are. After all these kids have been through? After all they've done and how far they've come, you're just giving up?"

"Who said they're giving up?" Peele asked, sneering at Seth.

"Yeah," Mr. Renfro said, "who said that?"

From his pocket, Mr. Renfro removed a silver whistle. He jiggled its lanyard, uncoiling it before dipping his head through the loop and allowing the whistle to hang just above his sloppy beer belly. Mr. Renfro became Coach Renfro right before their eyes.

Seth turned to Mr. Flee and said, "This guy walked out on these kids. When it looked like they weren't going to the playoffs, he quit."

"I never quit anything!" Coach Renfro bellowed. "That was a coaching technique."

"For motivation," Jamie said, spitting the words at Troy.

"Then this . . . this gorilla," Coach Renfro said, stabbing his finger at Seth and looking at Peele, who had begun to jot down notes, "he just jumped in and turned a couple parents against me and took *my* team through the playoffs."

Seth's face turned dark.

"Mr. Flee," he said, "you can take this up with my lawyer tomorrow."

Seth stood staring Flee down until the man dropped his eyes. Then, breathing hard through clenched teeth, he turned to Renfro, pointed at the parking lot, and said, "Get off this field. I've got practice. It's not *my* team. It's not *your* team. It's the kids' team, and they've worked too hard and done too much to have it taken away from them. We're going to win that game Saturday night. We're going to be champions, so get out of here.

"We've got work to do."

For a moment, everyone stood as still as statues, but when Officer Cussing's hand crept slowly around the handle of his pistol, Troy let out a gasp.

CHAPTER THIRTY-ONE

EVERYONE FOLLOWED TROY'S GAZE, startled at the sight of Officer Cussing. The young cop looked down with the rest of them at the hand he'd wrapped around the pistol grip as if his arm belonged to another person. With his other hand, he slapped the right hand off the gun, then reached for the other side of his belt, snapping free a walkie-talkie and raising it to his mouth.

"Suzie," he said into the small black brick, "this is Officer Cussing requesting backup, over."

The radio beeped and scratched and a voice said, *"Leonard, where are you at? I got your twenty as the Junior Football League practice fields. What on earth do you need backup for?"*

"I got a big NFL player resisting arrest," Cussing

said into the walkie-talkie. "Seth Halloway."

"Who told you to arrest anybody?"

"Well, Suzie," Cussing said, beginning to whine, his eyes flickering between them all, "I got an issue arising here and I need some backup."

"You don't need backup," Seth said in a low tone of disgust and threw his hands up in the air. "I'm not resisting anything. You people want to mess this thing up for these kids, go ahead. Have fun. I hope you choke on it."

Seth left, his strides obviously causing him pain.

"You choke on it, Halloway," Peele said, raising his voice. "And choke on what I write about you tomorrow, too."

Seth spun around and took a step toward Peele, who cringed and ducked behind the chubby young cop.

"You can write what you like," Seth said. "You're still trash, Peele. That's all you and your little split lip ever were. That's all you ever will be."

This time, Seth marched away without stopping.

Coach Renfro snorted in disgust, then turned toward the assembled players and tooted his whistle. "All right, enough drama. Get lined up for stretching!"

The players stood and muttered among themselves.

"Get going!" Coach Renfro screamed. "You know what to do! Or you'll run laps till you puke!"

Jamie ran out in front of the lines and hollered to

get everyone started on a set of jumping jacks. The two assistant coaches looked at each other, then at Coach Renfro.

"Let's go," Coach Renfro ordered as he marched past them. "I'm not holding any grudges for what you two did, but I'm not taking any crap from you, either."

"What about them?" asked one of the coaches, pointing at Troy, Nathan, and Tate.

Coach Renfro spun around, studying them for a moment before he said, "You three want to play, that's okay with me. Hughes and McGreer, you'll stay put right where you are, but you can forget being team captains. That's for real players. White, you're backup quarterback now, same thing as during the regular season."

Coach Renfro's mouth twisted up into a smirk, and he said, "But as a reward for helping this team out over the last few weeks, I figured I'll let you be the holder on PATs and field goals, get you a little playing time in the championship game under the lights. That's *if* you don't give me any trouble."

Troy turned to his friends. Nathan looked down at the grass, nudging a divot into the dirt with the toe of his cleat. Tate looked up at Troy, her eyes swimming in tears yet to fall.

"You guys stay," Troy said, his throat choking out the words. "Really, I mean it. Don't miss the game because of me."

Troy turned before they could answer, shouted for

Seth to wait up, and jogged off the field in the direction of the H2. He didn't want them to see his own tears of anger and anguish, so he didn't turn around until he got to the big yellow SUV. When he did, what he saw shocked him.

CHAPTER THIRTY-TWO

NO LESS THAN TWENTY feet behind him, Tate and Nathan jogged along, scuffing the dry grass. They grinned at Troy as if they'd won the lottery. Behind them, kicking up a cloud of dust that glimmered in the golden light of the setting sun, were nearly twenty players, led by Rusty Howell—more than half the rest of the team.

Beyond them, the ones who remained closed their ranks beneath a tirade of shouting from Coach Renfro.

"Hey, guys?" Troy said, biting back his smile. "You sure? You might not get a chance like this again, playing on TV. It's the state championship."

Tate said, "If I ever want to make a fool of myself in front of thousands of people, I'll sing 'She Bangs' on *American Idol*."

Rusty Howell walked up and said, "I hear that. You

couldn't get goofier than going out there against Valdosta with Jamie Renfro at quarterback."

"And his dad coaching," Nathan said. "That could win *World's Funniest Pet Videos.* The guy's a mutt."

"Man," Troy said, glaring out at the field, "this whole thing *stinks.*"

Rusty shrugged and headed across the parking lot, where his dad stood next to the open door of his car, wearing a suit and holding his hands in the air to signal that he wondered what was going on. The rest of the kids filtered through the lot as well, some of them sharing cell phones to call for rides from their parents. Seth waited for Troy, Nathan, and Tate to climb into the H2 before he fired up the engine and pulled out of his spot. On the way out of the lot, Rusty's dad flagged Seth down. Seth lowered his window and explained what had happened.

Rusty's dad wrinkled his forehead in disbelief, then shot a glance over at the field and said, "From the beginning, I worried about Rusty playing for that guy. I'm sorry, Seth. Listen, let me get the parents together and see what I can do."

"My dad's a lawyer," Rusty said from the front seat of his car.

"Are you?" Seth asked. "My agent's a lawyer. I was going to call him, but you being a father, I think that would be better."

The father shrugged and said, "An environmental

lawyer, really, but I think I can help with this."

"Well," Seth said, "it'll have to be fast. If we're going to have a chance Saturday, we need to practice."

"Give me until tomorrow evening," Rusty's father said.

They shook hands and Seth pulled away, driving in silence. After he dropped off Nathan and Tate, he pulled up into the dirt patch in front of Troy's house. Seth turned off the engine and sat there with his hands on the wheel.

"You didn't do what they said, did you?" Troy asked, his words barely rising above the sound of the ticking engine.

Seth looked at him for a minute, then sighed and said, "Troy, I told you, the only shot I ever took from Gumble was a vitamin shot. There's nothing illegal about it. Nothing at all."

"I know," Troy said, smiling. "Come in, okay?"

Seth nodded his head. They went in and sat down on the couch next to Troy's mom.

"Well," she said quietly after listening to the whole story, "maybe Mr. Howell can do something. There's nothing more we can do. Some things are just meant to be."

"Mr. Langan and Coach McFadden said the NFL is coming in to test me for steroids," Seth said. "If I clear that—which I will—then I'll be set to play Sunday, but it won't help us in getting ready for the Tigers' championship game. I need to be with the team. We've got a lot of work to do if we're going to stand a chance. Meanwhile, the whole world thinks I'm dirty, and I have to just sit here.

"I want to *do* something," Seth said, curling his hands into fists and slowly rapping a knuckle against his own forehead. "That's what I love about this stupid game: You can always do something. You can work harder. You can lift more weights. You can watch more film. You can run more sprints. There's no politics, no who said what to who and why. Football is pure. You win or you lose because you're better. Now I just feel so helpless. I feel like, like . . ."

"Like everyone else?" Troy said.

"I guess," Seth said.

His mom sat rubbing big circles on Seth's back before she said, "I got a call from Cecilia."

"Great," Seth said sarcastically.

"She wanted to make sure I was clear on their suggestion not to do any interviews and not to let anyone talk to Troy," his mom said.

"Who wants to talk to me?" Troy asked, suddenly remembering his chance for fame and thinking of Jamie Renfro's face if he saw Troy on TV with Larry King or some other famous person.

"Apparently a lot of people," his mom said. "It's a good thing our phone number isn't listed or I bet they'd start showing up at the door. ESPN is doing a segment on the whole scandal—that's what they're calling it now, a scandal—on the halftime show of *Monday Night Football*."

"Scandal?" Seth asked.

"Because Peele is saying the Falcons are stealing other teams' signals," Troy's mom said.

"I wonder if that's the only scandal they'll be talking about," Seth said, his face grim.

"Well," Troy asked, looking from the silent TV to Seth, "are we going to watch?"

The clock on the wall ticked.

Silence fell around them like a heavy snow.

Finally, Seth cleared his throat.

CHAPTER THIRTY-THREE

"I GUESS WE MIGHT as well see how bad the damage really is," Seth said, settling back into his seat.

As the game got under way, the announcers made an occasional reference to the Falcons "scandal" and how they'd be exploring the story during halftime. That's as much as they said, though, so Troy, Seth, and Tessa got quieter and more uncomfortable as the game slowly crept toward its midpoint. Troy needed to use the bathroom, but he didn't want to move.

When halftime finally came, the walls seemed to have closed in on them and Troy couldn't wait to use the bathroom any longer. He jumped out of his seat at the sight of a commercial. By the time he got back, Seth and his mom were sitting on the edges of their seats, their mouths hanging open, their eyes wide, staring at the TV.

The announcer finished saying something Troy didn't catch, he only heard Seth's name. Then, filling the television screen, appeared the face of Brent Peele.

"Joining us now from Atlanta," the announcer said, "is Mr. Brent Peele, investigative reporter for the *Atlanta Journal-Constitution* and the writer breaking the story of how the Falcons' recent playoff run may involve not only cheating but steroid use."

"Also joining us from Atlanta," the announcer said as the screen split, showing the face of another guest beside Peele, "is Doctor Clive Gumble."

Troy's mom glanced at Seth and said, "Oh my God."

CHAPTER THIRTY-FOUR

TROY COULDN'T MOVE. HE simply stood there, watching the men on the TV as they talked. Somewhere in the back of his mind, Troy realized that it wasn't just for him that the image of Seth Halloway was being destroyed. The entire country watched *Monday Night Football.* Fans of Seth Halloway, fans of the Falcons, fans of the very game itself would be feeling the same sickening knot in their stomach as Troy was feeling now.

At one point, the announcer asked, "Mr. Peele, how surprised are you that a player with a reputation like Seth Halloway's might be involved in something like this?"

"I'm not surprised at all," Peele said. "I've always known a different side of Seth Halloway. I actually used to play football myself with Halloway at Marist, until he hit me with a cheap shot that ended my career. Also, I remembered from my days at Marist that Seth Halloway actually admitted to using steroids in college."

"*Admitted* it?" the announcer asked, obviously shocked.

"That's right," Peele said. "Even though most NFL fans don't know it, Halloway admitted using steroids in an interview with the *Poughkeepsie Journal* in 1997."

"An admitted juicer," the announcer said, shaking his head. "Dr. Gumble? Is it true that you've given Seth Halloway steroid injections?"

"I'm not proud of what I've done," Gumble said, looking sad, "but I fell on hard times and Seth Halloway paid me a lot of money to give him those injections."

When Peele and Gumble had finished smearing Seth and branding him a cheater and a drug user, the NFL commissioner appeared from a studio in New York.

"The NFL takes all such accusations very seriously," Commissioner Roger Goodell said. "We have already begun investigating allegations into the Falcons' improper use of electronic equipment and computers to steal signals from other teams, and we will, of course, expand that investigation now to see what truth there may be to the allegations of steroid use."

When asked just how serious the league was about the allegations, the commissioner furrowed his eyebrows, stared into the camera, and said, "Serious enough for me to get on an airplane for Atlanta first thing tomorrow morning."

The announcer thanked the commissioner, and the TV went to another commercial. Troy's mom raised the remote and flicked off the television. For the second time that night, Troy heard the tick of the clock on the wall as if it were a time bomb.

"Seth?" Troy's mother finally said.

Seth sat next to her on the couch, bent forward with his head down. Troy's mom said his name again, this time in a disappointed whisper, and he looked up slowly.

"In college?" she asked.

Seth laughed abruptly, shook his head, and said, "I had knee surgery. I got a staph infection, and they gave me steroids to help the swelling and the infection. That's it. That's my steroid use. It was completely medical, not for getting stronger."

"But the way Peele made it sound . . ." Troy's mom said.

"What?" Seth asked, struggling to his feet. "You're not telling me you believe them? That piece of trash Peele and that quack Gumble?"

Troy's mom put her fingertips to her closed mouth and looked as if she might cry. "Of course not."

Troy couldn't help the way he looked at Seth. He couldn't help wondering if Seth hadn't lied.

"But you said you *never* took them," Troy said, the words gushing from his mouth without him even thinking.

Seth wheeled on him, a look of surprise on his face as if he hadn't known Troy was in the room.

His voice came out eerily calm. "I told you, Troy. I never used them. I meant used them for strength training, for cheating. When you get them from a doctor after surgery, that's not cheating. That's medicine. People do that all the time. They're twisting this thing, twisting the truth, same as Peele did with you."

"We've got to tell people," Troy's mom said.

"And we will," Seth said. "We'll do our best, but you know as well as I do that sometimes the truth doesn't matter."

"I thought the truth always comes out," Troy said.

"Not always," Seth said. "Not with the media, and sometimes, even when it does finally come out, it's too late. The damage is done."

"You mean your career?" Troy asked.

"Maybe that," Seth said, nodding, "but I was thinking about my reputation."

"But if you're innocent?" Troy's mom said.

"You'd think that matters," Seth said, "but it doesn't. I took this psychology class in college once. They found that when people heard something outrageous, even after they later knew it to be false, when you asked them a few years later? The outrageous lie is what they remembered as the truth. The damage Peele's doing to me is permanent.

"But that doesn't mean we're not going to fight this. I'll do what I can with the Falcons and the league, and if Rusty's dad can get the parents together tomorrow night and get me back as your coach, then we'll fight for that, too."

CHAPTER THIRTY-FIVE

BY TUESDAY AFTERNOON, RUSTY'S dad had contacted the parents of every Duluth Tigers team member as well as the entire Duluth Junior Football League board of directors and had given them his lawyerly pitch about Seth being innocent until *proven* guilty. The president, Mr. Flee, had agreed that the best thing for everyone would be to meet immediately before practice that night and decide by vote, once and for all, just who would coach the Tigers in Saturday's state championship game.

As they pulled to a stop in the parking lot, riding high in Seth's H2, Troy could see, standing in the middle of the group of adults who had gathered by the bleachers, not only Jamie Renfro and his dad, looking mean, but, right beside them, Brent Peele.

"Seth," Troy said, pointing.

"I know," Seth said, his face grim as he climbed out of the truck. "Come on. Let's go do this."

CHAPTER THIRTY-SIX

THE SHADOWS HAD DEEPENED to pools of black, but a warmer-than-normal day left the air pleasant, even though the field's lights had already been turned on so they could practice into the twilight. Nearly a hundred people crowded around the bleachers. Mr. Flee stood next to Rusty's dad and held up his hands for everyone to be quiet, asking them all to take a seat in the bleachers. The league president wore a gray suit, again with a crisp white shirt, and a brilliant yellow tie. The flap of hair that covered his shiny head lifted on the twilight breeze and waved like a small flag, but no one was in the mood to laugh.

"We all know why we're here," Flee said, flattening the hair back down on his scalp, "and I want to thank Mr. Howell for looking into this so we can work it out without lawsuits or anything crazy like that. What the board has decided to do is to let both coaches say what they have to say and then take a vote. And we're hopeful that whoever we decide on as coach, the entire team will play in the game on Saturday. This is the first time a Duluth team has made it to the state championship, and it would be a shame if the team didn't have the full squad to compete."

"You tell *him* that!" Jamie Renfro's father yelled, jumping up from his seat in the front row and pointing at Seth, who sat on the other end of the bleachers with Troy and his mom. "He's the one who made half the team quit!"

Seth jumped up, too, and said, "That's a lie!"

"You calling me a liar?" Renfro shouted.

"If the shoe fits!" Seth said.

"STOP IT!"

Everyone froze. Standing beside Mr. Flee and Mr. Howell was Tate's mom, Mrs. McGreer, a short, stout woman with a red face and a concrete scowl. She kept her hair in a big tight bun and could quote passages from the Bible with more force and ease than a Sunday-morning TV preacher.

"We *will* have a debate," Mrs. McGreer said, "and then we *will* have a vote. I've got a prayer meeting to attend to, and I'm sure the rest of us have things to do, too. 'The bread of deceit is sweet to a man, but afterward his mouth shall be filled with gravel.' Proverbs

20:17. So let's hear both sides—without interruptions—and make up our minds. And don't you give *me* a dirty look, Mr. Renfro. I'm not one of your players, and I'm not afraid of you. I don't give a shiitake mushroom about your dirty looks."

Mrs. McGreer never swore, but she always got her point across as if she cursed like a rapper, and when she did, Troy—like every other kid around—couldn't help giggling, no matter how serious the situation. Mrs. McGreer followed up her shiitake mushroom comment by planting her fists on her hips and taking a step toward Coach Renfro, who immediately sat back down. Seth sat down, too.

Mrs. McGreer turned to Mr. Flee, handed him a quarter from her purse, and said, "I suggest we flip a coin to decide who goes first."

Flee took the coin, nodded, and said, "Heads, Seth Halloway goes first; tails, it's Coach Renfro."

Flee flipped the coin. "Tails. Coach Renfro, you have five minutes to speak."

Coach Renfro got up. He was wearing tight blue coaching shorts, a white cap, and a big gray Dallas Cowboys sweatshirt that partially disguised his beer belly. A silver whistle dangled from his neck.

"I only got a couple things to say," Coach Renfro began, grumbling. "Then I'm gonna let someone else use what time I got left to let you all know a couple things about Mr. Seth Halloway that'll make you want me to be your kids' coach even more."

Coach Renfro hitched up his snug shorts and said, "First off, Halloway is an admitted steroid user. We all know that now, and that's not the kind of person who should be coaching our kids. Second, I coached this team all season until Seth Halloway jumped in and stole it out from under me."

A murmur went up through the crowd, some agreeing with Coach Renfro, some definitely not.

"I know I'm no big-shot NFL player," Coach Renfro said. "In a way, that's not so good, but in another way it's real good. I'm a father, just like all of you, and I'm a respectable person whose face isn't plastered all over the papers because I'm some juicer."

Out of the corner of his eye, Troy saw his mom stiffen. A growl crept up out of Seth's throat like a mad dog's, but Troy's mom gripped his hand and Seth kept his seat.

"So I should be the coach for this game," Coach Renfro said with a curt nod. "And you should listen to what Mr. Peele here has to say before you think about what's right and what's best for these kids."

Peele jumped out of his seat and Coach Renfro sat down, folding his arms across his chest with great satisfaction.

"I've known Seth Halloway for fifteen years," Peele said, looking around at everyone but Seth, Troy, and his mom. "And I know the truth about him. Most of you have read the truth in my newspaper: He's not the hero people used to think he was. Instead of being someone our kids can look up to, Seth Halloway has become a symbol of what's wrong in sports, of trying to win at all costs, even if it means cheating."

Seth's leg shook and he leaned forward in his seat. He gritted his teeth and his jaw muscles rippled. Troy's mom locked her arm through his elbow to hold him back.

"Drug use happens in sports," Peele said, frowning. "It's unfortunate, but it's true. What would be even worse, though, is if this group of parents allowed these young athletes to think that it's okay, that you can use something like steroids and get away with it. If you don't vote for Coach Renfro to coach this team, I'm afraid of what your own kids might do as they grow up into high school athletes. As many as six hundred thousand high school kids in this country today use steroids. I think you're all decent people, and if you use your instincts, I know you're going to want to protect these kids."

Peele sat down, and Flee nodded at Seth. Troy's mom let go of his arm and Seth stood up, walking to the middle of the bleachers before turning to face the crowd.

CHAPTER THIRTY-SEVEN

"FIRST THINGS FIRST," SETH said. "I have never used steroids illegally and I never will. This . . ."

Seth stabbed a finger at Peele so hard the reporter flinched.

". . . person, I guess I have to call him," Seth said, "even though he's a lying *rat*, is trying to ruin my NFL career. Why, you might ask? Because of something that happened between us a long time ago that's got nothing to do with any of this, and also I guess it's because I'm doing something he always wanted to do but never could. Either way, I am taking a test tomorrow that will show everyone I am completely clean. That *will* happen and my name *will* be cleared. In the meantime, if we're going to win Saturday, I've got to get these kids practicing."

"Maybe you're clean *now*," Peele said. "Maybe it's out of your system."

"That's enough!" Mrs. McGreer said, jumping up and sticking her face into Peele's personal space. "He let you have your say; now you'll let him have his!"

Mrs. McGreer popped back into her seat as quickly as she had popped up. She smoothed her skirt and nodded at Seth.

"If I'm not cleared by Friday," Seth said, "if they don't say I'm *totally* clean—which I am—then I'll resign and Renfro can coach this team on Saturday. He can use my plays and my playbook, the same one that got them to the championship. You can't ask for better than that."

Seth stopped talking and looked at Troy, offering up a wink. Troy gave Seth a thumbs-up. His mom put a hand on Troy's knee and squeezed.

"Finally," Seth said, "Mr. Renfro quit on this team."

"Not true!" Coach Renfro screamed.

"Sit *down*," Tate's mom hollered, swinging her purse and clumping Coach Renfro in the butt with it.

Coach Renfro glared at her, rubbing his backside, but sat down when he saw the rest of the parents scowling at him and shaking their heads.

"It's true," Seth said. "That's how I ended up coaching these kids in the first place. He was going to forfeit the last game because some parents had complained about his coaching tactics and the team looked like it was out of the playoffs, so he quit. When I took the job,

I had no idea that we'd get into the playoffs. No one did. But here we are, and not because of Mr. Renfro. He even gave our playbook to the Dunwoody Dragons, hoping they'd knock us out of the playoffs. Heck, the only thing he knows less about than football is kids. You think this team would have won these past weeks without Troy at quarterback?"

Troy's face heated up and he looked down at his football cleats, scuffing them against the dirt.

"We couldn't have won without him," Seth said. "And this team can't win without him Saturday, either. So let's get this vote done and get going so we can run some plays together before it gets too late."

Seth sat down, and Mr. Flee passed out ballots on small squares of green paper.

"We have thirty-eight kids on the team," Mr. Flee said, "and I've got a ballot for each kid's parents. There's only one vote for each player, so you parents will have to decide together on how your family wants to vote. The one requirement we have for your vote is that you agree your child will play in Saturday's game no matter what the result. So, if you vote, your kid plays. No exceptions."

Some of the parents talked in urgent whispers among themselves, but most checked a name without saying a thing, folded the paper, and dropped it into the box Mr. Flee carried through the stands.

Troy's mom checked Seth's name on her ballot and

held it up in front of Troy's face.

"You okay with this?" she asked. "If we vote, you play, even if Coach Renfro wins."

Troy glanced over and saw Jamie Renfro sneering at him. He wondered how he could ever get through the next few days if he had to be Jamie's backup. But the only thing worse than that would be if Seth lost the vote because Troy and Tate and even Nathan didn't agree to play under Coach Renfro. Troy sneered right back at Jamie, then nodded to his mom as she dropped her ballot into the box.

Troy watched carefully as Flee unfolded the ballots one by one, sorting them out in different piles as he went. It amazed Troy that anyone could have voted for Coach Renfro until he realized that some people simply didn't believe Seth. And as both stacks of green ballots grew, Troy knew that what Seth had said to his mom in the living room the night before was true: The damage from the newspaper would be permanent, whether Seth was proven innocent or not.

Finally, Mr. Flee counted each pile of ballots, then put them back into the box, looked up, and cleared his throat to speak.

CHAPTER THIRTY-EIGHT

"I'D LIKE TO ASK the players to get together out on the field with all their gear," Mr. Flee said. "Because after I announce who the coach is, you'll all need to get to work as a team. Parents, you're welcome to watch from the stands, but please don't interfere. We'll get these kids going again and we'll stay out of it. The vote is done. They're all counted, and the decision is final."

Mr. Flee paused to look at Mrs. McGreer. She gave one solid nod and the league president said, "Okay. Kids? Take the field."

Troy looked at his mom and she shooed him toward the fifty-yard line. Troy got up and walked out onto the grass, turning to look at the adults in the stands and the back of Mr. Flee's shiny head with its waving flap of hair. Tate stood next to him and touched his arm. Nathan walked over and held out his hand. Troy slapped him five.

"So," Mr. Flee said, clearing his throat one final time and tugging at the collar of his shirt as if to loosen his tie. "The Tigers' coach will be Seth Halloway."

Troy and Nathan and Tate jumped in the air and cheered, along with most of the other kids. Mr. Renfro stormed past Mr. Flee, bumping him in the shoulder—almost knocking him down. He grabbed Jamie by the arm and dragged him off toward the parking lot.

"Mr. Renfro," Mr. Flee called after him in a weak voice, "we had an agreement."

Without turning around, Mr. Renfro flipped his middle finger in the air and kept walking.

Peele stood calmly.

As Seth walked past him and toward the players, Peele said, "Enjoy your little victory, Halloway, because junior league football is all you're going to have left by the time I'm finished."

Seth glanced over his shoulder, let out a little laugh, and said, "Peele, why don't you write something you know about, like the inside of a trash can."

Troy and his friends giggled, but instead of joining in, Seth blew his whistle and hollered at his team to take two laps, then line up for stretching.

By the time Seth blew the final whistle, signaling an end to practice, Troy didn't know which hurt him more, his legs or his brain. Not only had they run more than fifty plays on offense as well as on defense, but Seth had insisted that they learn every play and every signal for Saturday's game. While Troy normally got to rest during the defensive part of practice, he now had to focus just as hard and hit more than he was used to in order to be ready to play strong safety.

His sweat-soaked clothes turned clammy and chill before he reached the H2 and crawled up into the backseat. Tate got in the other side. Troy's mom had spent her time during practice in the front seat, reading a book by the dome light, and she looked up when Troy slammed the door shut.

"How'd it go?" his mom asked.

Troy got stuck trying to slip out of his shoulder pads. Tate reached over to help, and he groaned.

"That bad?" his mom asked.

"He's trying to kill us," Troy said.

Seth climbed in behind the wheel and turned around, grinning. "Rough night, huh, champ?"

"I can barely lift my arms," Troy said.

"Seth, I hope you're not going to exhaust them too much," his mom said. "They have to play a game on Saturday."

"Gotta do it," Seth said, starting the engine. "That's how it goes in the NFL. As far as practices go, four days before a game is the toughest day of the week. You get your whole game plan in. You do your hitting.

Tomorrow will be tough, too, but a little easier. Then the last two days before the game it's all mental work. Trust me, I know what I'm doing. He'll be all right. We'll ice him down in the tub and give him some ibuprofen."

"Ice in what tub?" Troy asked.

Seth glanced at him and said, "The bathtub. We fill it with cold water and ice and in you go."

Troy shivered at the thought of it.

"That makes you feel better?" Troy asked.

"Hurts like heck at first," Seth said, "but after a few minutes, you numb up and it's pretty good for you. You'll be like new by Saturday."

"Saturday?" Troy said. "What about the rest of the week?"

CHAPTER THIRTY-NINE

TROY ACHED FROM HEAD to toe the next morning. The memory of the icy tub made him break out in goose bumps all over again. He crawled out of bed, staggered to the bathroom, then limped into the kitchen, where his mom worked at the stove. When Troy saw Seth at the table, he froze, wondering what news the paper had for them today.

"What's it say?" Troy asked.

Seth peered over the top, then flipped the pages until Troy could see the sports section headline: DIRTY BIRD.

"Wow," Troy said. "Is that about you?"

"Yup," Seth said, turning the pages and disappearing behind the paper again. "The fun continues."

"You came for breakfast?" Troy asked.

"That, and I figured I'd stop by before practice to see

how my star quarterback is doing," Seth said, dropping the paper again. "You okay?"

"Yeah," Troy said. "A little sore is all. A lot sore, actually."

"That happens," Seth said. "You need to take some of that ibuprofen."

"I put two next to your juice glass," Troy's mom said, flipping eggs onto their plates.

Troy swallowed the pills and said, "Seth said if I was real bad I should take three or four."

"Three or four isn't good for your stomach," his mom said.

"Seth said—"

"I'm your mom," she said, cutting him off.

Seth looked like he was going to say something, then winked at Troy, shook his head, and disappeared behind the paper again.

Since his mom wasn't going into work, Seth drove Troy to school on his way to Flowery Branch. During the drive, Troy asked, "Why didn't you just tell her about the ibuprofen? You know more about it than she does."

"Like she said, she's your mom," Seth said, glancing at Troy from behind a pair of dark sunglasses as he turned the big H2 into the school driveway, "and she's a good one, too. I had a pretty good mom myself, but not like yours. No, no. One thing I'm not going to do is come between you two. You're my man, Troy, but you want backup when you're going at it with your mom? Don't look to me. I'm smarter than that."

Troy wrinkled his nose and Seth laughed.

"What's it like living in a mansion?" Troy asked, the words escaping his mouth like kids busting out of the school's front doors at the end of the day.

Seth looked at him blankly, then a smile curled the corners of his lips. "You like my place?"

"It's awesome," Troy said.

"Thanks," Seth said. "I worked hard to get it. I paid for it with my blood and bones. It didn't come cheap and it didn't come easy."

"I'm going to work hard, too," Troy said.

"I know that," Seth said. "I see."

"If we win this game," Troy said, "I figure I'm on my way. Who needs ten thousand a week from the Falcons? In a few years, I'll be famous and making millions like you, and I'll get me and my mom a house in Cotton Wood and a fancy car, maybe a Benz."

"Sounds good," Seth said, "but I don't think you have to do something like that for your mom. She'd be pretty crazy about you no matter what you did, no matter where you lived or what kind of car you drove. That's what I like best about her. Those things don't matter to her."

"But she should have them if I make it to the NFL," Troy said. "You've got them."

"I know I do, and I enjoy them," Seth said. "But they're not *necessary*. That's not what makes you happy."

"But being famous does, right?" Troy said.

"I doubt it," Seth said. "I'm not so famous, anyway."

"You are, kind of."

"Well, no matter how much fame you have, it all ends sooner or later," Seth said, "and then you're left with yourself, who you are, and the people who really love you. That's what matters."

Troy closed his mouth and stared straight ahead.

"I could see you playing in the NFL though, Troy," Seth said, pulling to a stop in front of the school. "You get a little luck and a little size, and I really could. Here you go."

Troy thanked Seth, hopped down from the big, shiny SUV, and glanced around the school yard. Sometimes Jamie Renfro got delivered to school in his mom's Jaguar, and no matter what Seth said about cars and mansions and fame, Troy wanted Jamie to see him arrive in style, too. He waved and shouted as Seth rumbled away, but when he glanced over his shoulder, no one seemed to have noticed. He walked slowly toward the doors, looking back at the buses until Tate and Nathan finally stepped off theirs. The two of them followed a twisting line of kids heading for the main entrance. Troy jogged over to them and explained about Seth giving him a ride and why he hadn't seen them on the bus.

"So, you didn't hear the news?" Nathan said.

Troy looked at Tate. She stared down at her feet and began to stir a small pebble around the asphalt with her toe.

"What news?" Troy asked.

CHAPTER FORTY

"EVERYONE'S TALKING ABOUT IT," Nathan said, his eyes bulging.

"What?" Troy asked, anger frosting the question, frustrated with the way Nathan was dragging things out.

"Jamie Renfro," Tate said.

"Jamie Renfro what?" Troy asked.

"The gloves are coming off!" Nathan said, unable to keep his voice from drawing stares all around as they made their way into the school and down the halls.

"What gloves?" Troy asked.

"Fight gloves," Nathan said. "Don't worry, I got your back. His buddies try to pull any funny stuff, they'll be getting a taste of this."

Troy stared at Nathan's fist for a moment before

saying, "What's with the fist?"

"Man, wake up. Jamie Renfro's calling you out," Nathan said. "You two are going to fight."

"No I'm not," Troy said.

Nathan's face fell. "You got to."

"Says who?" Troy asked.

"Man, he's talking about you," Nathan said.

"So what?"

"So, he keeps saying things," Nathan said.

"I don't care."

"Troy, you can't just let him keep dissing you," Nathan said.

"Who cares what he says?" Troy said, passing through the entrance and into the main hall. "He can say what he wants."

"But he's *saying* he's going to fight you," Nathan said, jogging to keep up.

Troy stopped short and Nathan bumped into him.

"I thought you want to be a champ," Troy said. "A state champ."

"So?" Nathan said, wrinkling his brow.

"What if I break my hand or twist my ankle fighting Jamie Renfro?" Troy asked.

"Troy's right," Tate said.

"Tate, who asked you?" Nathan said. "You're a girl."

"Don't start *that*," Tate said, growling and poking Nathan in the chest with her finger.

"Well," Nathan said in a mutter, "you guys are going

to make us all look bad if you let Jamie Renfro keep saying stuff and you just let it go. I don't know what good it does being a football champ if everyone is calling you a chicken."

"Chicken?" said a nasty voice. "Who's the chicken?"

Troy, Tate, and Nathan spun around to see Jamie Renfro standing there with two of the goons he called friends.

"You're not talking about Troy White?" Jamie said. "White, like white meat on a chicken?"

"Come on," Troy said to his friends, turning to go.

"Yeah," Jamie said, "I'd walk away too if I were you."

"I am."

"Just make sure you meet me after seventh period in the locker room," Jamie said. "'Cause that's where you and I are going to settle this."

"I'm not settling anything," Troy said, continuing to walk.

He, Tate, and Nathan were halfway down the hall when Jamie shouted, "That's right, go run to your groupie mama."

"What?" Troy said, freezing in his tracks. "What did he say?"

"Troy, come on," Tate said, taking his arm. "Like you said, who cares?"

"Groupie?" Troy said, the color red flashing in his eyes. "You must be talking about your own mom."

"My mom?" Jamie said, laughing and nudging his friends. "Your mom is the NFL groupie chasing after Seth Halloway. I guess he went for her because he's so old and the magic is gone for him, but I heard the one she really wanted was John Abraham. He's got a bigger contract."

"*You*," Troy said, clenching his fists and his teeth and moving fast toward Jamie Renfro.

"Fight. Fight. Fight," the kids all around them in the crowded hall began to chant.

Troy went right for Jamie, his fist cocked and ready to throw a punch right at Jamie's mouth. But before Troy got there, someone, maybe one of Jamie's buddies, or maybe just some anxious bystander, tripped him. Troy tumbled forward as he threw his punch. His fist sang through the air, grazing Jamie's nose and twisting Troy sideways so that when he fell, his head banged into the door of an open locker. He crashed to the floor, faceup, and the back of his head struck the solid surface.

Troy saw stars, then everything went black.

CHAPTER FORTY-ONE

TROY CAME TO IN a cloud of breath laced with the nauseating smell of decay and old coffee. Ms. Finkle, the vice principal, patted his cheek and asked over and over if he was okay. She helped Troy sit up and escorted him to the nurse's office, gripping him by the arm and delivering him to the exam table more like a prisoner than a patient.

"Hit his head in a fight," Ms. Finkle said to the nurse.

Troy used to feel bad for the rigid, middle-aged administrator. Kids called her the Fink or Funky Fink if they got a whiff of her breath. But now the sharp look on her face and the accusing glare of her small, dark eyes behind those cold wire-framed glasses left Troy with the urge to tell her to her face what kids called her behind her back.

He forgot about the Fink, though, when he heard the sound—a ringing, buzzing sound that reminded him of the time Nathan lit off a firecracker too close to Troy's head.

"What's that?" Troy asked the nurse.

She gave him a kind but puzzled look as she slipped a thermometer into his mouth. "What's what?"

"That noise," Troy said, looking around, his words garbled by the thermometer.

"I don't hear any noise," the nurse said.

"That buzz," Troy said.

"No more of your shenanigans," the Fink said, pointing a long finger at Troy. "Who were you fighting with?"

Troy worked his jaw to disperse the ringing. No matter how much he hated Jamie Renfro, he wasn't going to be a rat. He shook his head and said, "There wasn't a fight."

"I heard 'fight,'" the Fink said, still pointing. "When I hear 'fight' and I see someone lying loopy on the floor, I know there was a fight."

"I . . ." Troy said, still working his jaw, trying to think over the annoying sound, "I tripped."

Since what he said was true, Troy looked right at her without blinking. The Fink moved closer, breathing on him, boring into his eyes with her own.

In a whisper that rode on the back of a rancid gust of

breath, she said, "I'll get to the bottom of this, and when I do, you better hope you're telling me the truth."

The Fink stomped out of the nurse's office.

"I'll call your mother," the nurse said, removing the thermometer and scowling.

"I have a temperature?" Troy asked.

"No, for the noise you're hearing," the nurse said.

"Uh, no," Troy said, thinking of how unhappy his mother would be and how lying to her—the way he did to the Fink—would be next to impossible. His mother would sniff him out in two seconds. "I'm fine."

"Not if you have ringing in your ears," the nurse said, flicking a penlight in his eyes.

"I don't," Troy said, shaking his head. "Not anymore. I'm good."

"You don't feel nauseous? Dizzy? Light-headed?" the nurse asked.

"No, no," Troy said, hopping off the table. "I'm good."

"Do you want to rest for a little while to make sure?" the nurse asked, pointing to a plastic bed partially hidden behind a curtain.

"No," Troy said. "I've got a math quiz I don't want to miss."

When the nurse didn't try to stop him, Troy hurried out of the office and down the nearly empty hallways to his class. The Fink was nowhere in sight; Troy saw her only once more during the day, prowling the lunch room and removing one of Jamie Renfro's buddies by the collar, presumably for questioning about the fight.

"The Fink is still on the prowl," Nathan said through a mouthful of Twinkie.

"If anyone talks about a fight, she'll call my mom for sure," Troy said. "And if that happens, you know my mom, she'll ground me for at least a week, and that means no championship game on Saturday."

"Come on. You didn't do anything," Nathan said. "Your mom's tough, but she's not like Saddam Hussein—crazy or anything like that."

"No, but my mom hates fighting, and once she flings out what my punishment will be," Troy said, "she won't go back on it. Remember when I burned that tire in the woods and it almost started a forest fire? I got two weeks for that and she wouldn't make an exception, even for Gramp's birthday dinner, even when he begged her."

"But this is the *championship*," Nathan said. "This is once in a lifetime. She wouldn't take that away from you, would she?"

CHAPTER FORTY-TWO

"SHE DOESN'T CARE," TROY said, shaking his head. "Believe me."

"First of all," Tate said, slurping the last bit of milk from her carton, "you weren't technically fighting."

"He tried," Nathan said, then dropped his head when they both scowled at him.

"And," Tate said, "if one of *us* isn't going to say anything—which we're not—Jamie and his creeps sure aren't. They're the ones who started it."

"Well, technically, Troy did," Nathan said.

They glared at him again, throwing daggers with their eyes.

"What?" Nathan asked. "I'm with you guys. I'm just saying, technically, Troy took the first swing."

"After Jamie insulted his *mom*," Tate said, her face reddening with anger.

"Yeah, but insults aren't the same as throwing a haymaker," Nathan said. "Stop it with the ugly looks, you guys. I'm just saying, the best thing for the Duluth Tigers is that *no one* talks to the Fink."

"How's the buzzing in your ears, anyway?" Tate asked.

"Still there," Troy said in a quiet voice.

"Maybe you should tell someone," Tate said with a worried look on her face.

"You want us to lose Saturday or what?" Nathan asked.

"If he's got a concussion or something," Tate said, "I don't want him to do anything stupid."

"Do you know how big the trophies are that we'll get if we win this thing?" Nathan asked.

"You'd let your friend risk permanent brain damage for a hunk of metal?" Tate asked.

"He says it's just a little buzzing is all," Nathan said.

Troy twirled a finger next to his ear. "It's not like I'm going to have permanent brain damage or anything. Remember when Nathan had those firecrackers and he held one too long before he threw it and it went off by my ear? It's like that. It took a couple days to stop, and I'm sure this will, too. It's no big deal."

The day went on and, to Troy's relief, the buzzing began to diminish. It was still hard to concentrate in math class, but he convinced himself it wasn't any big deal. That changed, though, when he got home from school and found out that Commissioner Goodell wanted to see him the very next day.

"Mr. Langan and Seth told him what you can do," Troy's mom said from where she worked next to the kitchen sink. "He wants to see it for himself."

"Sure," Troy said, sitting down at the table with a plate of cookies and a glass of cold milk. "How? Watch some film?"

"No," his mom said, sliding a chicken into the oven and turning to face him. "The Cowboys and the Giants play tomorrow night in the Thursday-night game on NBC. Evidently, the commissioner and Mr. Langan want you to watch the game on TV with them at the Falcons offices. What do you think?"

Even though his mouth was empty, Troy swallowed.

The buzz was now gone from his brain, but a dull headache remained and, if the damage he did to his brain made the afternoon math lesson hard to figure, he had a bad feeling that it might do the same thing to his ability to predict plays.

"If I do show him I can really do this, will he let me keep working for the Falcons?" Troy asked.

"He might, but they're not making any promises," his mom said, wiping her hands on a dishtowel. "But at least it will prove that we didn't do anything illegal or against the rules."

"But if they won't promise to let me help the team, why should I show him what I can do?" Troy asked, scowling and setting the cookie down without taking a bite.

"Troy, I don't want to put pressure on you," his mom said as she dropped the towel into the sink and turned his way, "but if you can't prove it, well . . . Seth, me, and you are all probably going to be banned from the NFL. For life."

CHAPTER FORTY-THREE

WHEN SETH CAME OVER after practice, the three of them sat down to dinner. Troy was thinking about his football career through the fog of his mild headache.

"Troy," his mom said, "I asked you twice to say grace. Are you okay?"

"Sure," Troy said. "Just thinking."

"Thinking?"

"Going over in my mind the plays we're going to run on Saturday," Troy said, inventing a story as smooth and slick as watermelon seeds.

"Did you study those sheets I gave you?" Seth asked.

Troy nodded. "Sure."

Seth didn't mention his NFL drug test during dinner, and when Troy's mom asked him how practice went, he shrugged and said that his backup got more repetitions with the starting defense than he did. Troy knew that meant that the coaches thought it was possible that Seth wouldn't play on Sunday. Troy couldn't bring himself to ask Seth if that was because of his aching knees or the drug test—or because Troy might not be sending the plays in to help Seth make up for his lack of speed due to injury and age.

Either way, the sense of having all the good things come unraveled—their championship game, the Falcons' playoff run—stuck in Troy's mind like a warm glob of chewing gum.

After dinner, Seth took Troy to the Tigers' practice.

Stretching and throwing passes during warm-ups and individual drills didn't bother Troy, but when they got to the part of practice where the whole team came together to run plays, Troy had trouble. It wasn't that he didn't know what to do, it was just that his headache—mild as it was—distracted him and made it hard to concentrate. While the pain wasn't severe, he couldn't get rid of the notion that someone was gently pressing a thumb into the back of his left eyeball. Once he started making mistakes, it seemed like the headache was all he could think about.

After Troy threw his third interception—a first in his young career—Seth took him off to the side. The NFL linebacker put his hands on Troy's shoulder pads and bent down so that their eyes were level, with Seth peering in through Troy's face mask.

"What's up, buddy?" Seth asked in a quiet voice.

Troy shook his head and his eyes began to fill up. He sniffed, looked away, and said, "Nothing."

"Something," Seth said gently.

"Just an off night, that's all," Troy said, fighting back the tears, part of him wanting desperately to tell Seth what was wrong. But if Seth told his mom, she'd think he had a concussion, and even if she didn't find out about him fighting, he knew she'd never let him play with a head injury no matter how mild. "I'll be fine."

"Okay," Seth said, nodding his head as he straightened himself. "That happens."

Seth blew his whistle and told the offense to huddle up.

Troy tried to focus, but the more he tried, the worse it got. Finally, Seth stopped calling pass plays. They ran a couple dozen running plays, mostly draws where the whole offense made it look like a pass—linemen stepping back, receivers running routes, and Troy dropping back into the pocket—before Troy handed the ball off to a running back.

When they began working on defense, it was even worse for Troy. Normally, he could look at the offensive formation and know the play. But distracted by the headache, he had a hard time just knowing if it would be a run or a pass. Seth didn't say anything, but he gave Troy a look of doubt and shook his head. On the way home he asked Troy again if everything was okay.

"I'm just distracted by tomorrow, the commissioner and all that, that's all," Troy said.

Seth nodded. "Sometimes you just have a crap day, but if you want to win this thing, we need you at one hundred percent. I got that game film from my reporter friend in Macon today at the complex. I watched a little of these guys and, honestly, our team isn't good enough to beat Valdosta without you doing your football genius thing."

"Well, I should be okay for Saturday," Troy said, silently hoping it would be true.

"Sure," Seth said, reaching over and patting his shoulder, "you're just a little nervous. That's understandable. It'll go away once the game starts. Everyone knows that first hit comes and bang, the butterflies are gone. You'll be fine. Let's stop by my house for a couple minutes. I need some clothes and I've got that Valdosta game film on a DVD. We can watch some of it in my basement."

"So we can see it on the big screen?" Troy asked. He'd seen the huge plasma TV in Seth's basement before.

"Not so much the big screen," Seth said, "but the DVD player I have. It's a special machine that lets you reverse it and run it in slow motion. It's like the ones they have at Flowery Branch, makes the tape easier to analyze."

Troy nodded.

When they got to Seth's big stone mansion, Seth went upstairs to gather his things. Troy waited on the sprawling deck out back, looking down at the granite pool and the towering old trees and smiling at the huge swatch of grass where he had stolen a football in the time before he ever even knew Seth.

When Seth came downstairs, he set a duffle bag full of clothes by the front door and said, "Come on."

Troy followed him downstairs. Seth put on the film. Troy watched and listened to Seth as he showed Troy what he could expect from the Valdosta Vipers on Saturday.

Finally, Seth paused the film and asked Troy, "You got any ideas from what you've seen so far?"

The ache persisted behind Troy's eyeball and his mouth went dry. He shook his head.

Seth stared at him and said, "'Cause you usually have some good ones. What's up with you, anyway?"

Troy *wanted* to tell Seth the truth, but he didn't know if he could. He opened his mouth to speak, wondering himself what words would come out.

CHAPTER FORTY-FOUR

"NOTHING," TROY SAID, AVOIDING Seth's eyes. "I think I'm just tired . . . and nervous. Nervous about the commissioner tomorrow."

"Oh," Seth said, waving his hand, "don't worry about that."

"But my mom said we'd all get banned," Troy said, watching Seth's face to see his reaction. "For life. That means I can't play in the NFL, even if I'm good enough."

"They're not going to ban you," Seth said, snorting and shaking his head.

"They're not?" Troy asked.

"Of course not," Seth said, rising from the couch and removing the DVD from the machine.

Troy breathed out, relaxing. "Oh, good."

"You're the real deal," Seth said. "He'll see that when you watch the game, and everything will be fine. Come on."

Troy couldn't bring himself to ask what would happen if he *couldn't* prove it. He followed the big line-backer up the stairs and out to the H2. They climbed in and headed for Troy's house. Troy chewed on his lip for a minute, then said, "Seth, did you ever get a concussion?"

"Sure," Seth said, glancing at him before returning his eyes to the road.

"No big deal, right?" Troy said.

Seth raised and lowered his eyebrows. "Everyone used to think that, but I'm not so sure."

"Why not?"

"Well," Seth said, "when you get a concussion, it's your brain's way of telling you to be careful. It used to be they'd ask you how many fingers they held up and if you were even close to being right, they'd send you back into the game. Not now. Now, they do all kinds of tests to make sure you're all better. Some guys who had a lot of concussions have had problems with their memory, so people are a lot more careful about it. I don't think it's a huge deal, as long as you're careful. What makes you ask?"

Seth furrowed his brow, glanced at Troy, and asked, "You didn't get hit in the head last week against Dun-woody, did you?"

"No," Troy said, glad he could tell the truth and still keep Seth in the dark.

"Good," Seth said, exhaling through tight lips, "'cause I doubt your mom would let you play this week if you did."

Troy said, "But even if I did—which I didn't, I promise—I'd be able to play after a week, right?"

"As long as the symptoms were all gone," Seth said slowly. "Yeah, you'd be okay with the doctors. I'm just saying about your mom; she's pretty cautious when it comes to you. I don't really blame her. Moms do that, especially when you're the only kid they've got. You sure you're okay?"

Troy forced a laugh and said, "Yeah, I'm just asking because I saw Joe Horn get that concussion last Sunday and I was wondering if he'll be able to play this weekend. I love Joe Horn."

"Yeah," Seth said, studying Troy with a curious look on his face, "a lot of people do."

When they got home, Troy went right to bed. Even though he lay for a long time worrying about the headache, the far-off moan of a freight train finally lulled him to sleep. As he drifted away, he had the clear sense that the next day would be as important as any in his entire life.

CHAPTER FORTY-FIVE

WHEN TROY WOKE UP on Thursday morning, the headache was only a shadow of what it had been. Even so, he had another poor practice that evening. Seth put his finger on the problem when he took Troy aside and said not to worry, that having to watch a game with the commissioner would be distracting to anyone.

"This commissioner thing will all be behind you tonight," Seth said. "Don't worry. You'll be ready to go for the game."

On the way to Flowery Branch, Troy worked his jaw and tried to convince himself that the headache was gone and that even if it wasn't, he hadn't done any damage to his brain. But while he could lie well enough to other people, he had a hard time lying to himself, and as they pulled into the front circle of the Falcons complex, his stomach began to clench and roll. Seth brought the H2 to a stop behind his mom's green VW Bug.

"Don't worry," Seth said, patting his back. "You'll be fine."

Troy nodded and tried to sound confident. "Oh, yeah. I know."

Troy's mom met them at the door and they all walked upstairs together. Inside the big wood-paneled conference room, a projection screen showed the beginning of the Thursday-night game. Mr. Langan and Commissioner Goodell sat in leather swivel chairs.

The commissioner stood up along with the owner. They all shook hands, and Troy searched the tan, boyish face of the commissioner for hints of favor, finding none. The commissioner wore a blue blazer over a striped shirt, with tan slacks and loafers. In his hand was an unopened bottle of water. His blond hair had a hint of red in it that Troy hadn't noticed on TV, and his blue eyes sparkled with intelligence and a wisdom that made Troy feel like even the best lie he ever told would be as obvious as a stop sign to this man.

"So," the commissioner said, cracking open the bottle, his eyes glittering at Troy, "Mr. Langan tells me I'm in for quite a show."

Troy blushed and nodded.

"Before we start," the commissioner said, "I'd like you to tell me how you do what it is they say you can do."

"It's like how we study tendencies," Seth said, cutting

in. "Every team does it, and if you study the numbers hard enough, you can sometimes predict what the other team is going to do based on down, distance, the players they put on the field, formations—all the variables."

The commissioner scratched his chin and said, "I'd like Troy to tell me how *he* does it. From what I hear, it's not by studying computer printouts."

Troy looked at Seth, who nodded for him to go ahead.

"Well," Troy said, swallowing, "I guess I can't really explain it. Seth talks about tendencies and all that, but it's a lot simpler than that. I just watch a game and after a little bit, I just *know*. It's . . . like the weather. You know how if a cold front is coming and it's hot and muggy out they can predict rain? It's something like that. Some people—like Gramp—they say they can *feel* the rain coming. That's me. I feel it."

"Troy's a savant," Troy's mom said. "A normal kid in every other way, except when it comes to the patterns and probabilities of predicting football plays. When it comes to that, he's a genius, like a supercomputer."

The commissioner snorted and shook his head, casting a doubtful look at Mr. Langan before letting out a big sigh.

"Okay, let's get this going," the commissioner said.

They all sat down and Troy let his eyes lock in on the screen, where the Cowboys were already kicking off. Eli Manning took the field and began a tactical advance, moving his team down the field with a combination of runs and play-action passes—where he'd fake the run but pop upright in the pocket to deliver a quick pass downfield. Troy forced himself to breathe, slow and steady, and to block all other thoughts from his mind. So much was at stake.

"Deep post to the Z," Troy said, the words coming from a place so deep inside him that the sound of his own voice made him jump.

His eyes darted from one adult to the other. Their heads turned to the front of the room at the same time. Up on the screen, Eli Manning took the snap and dropped straight back into the pocket. The linemen blocked and the receivers raced downfield. The receiver at the top of the TV screen—the Z—went straight for twelve yards before breaking at a forty-five-degree angle toward the middle of the field in a post pattern.

Eli threw a bullet pass. The receiver snagged it from the air before being flattened by Cowboys' safety Roy Williams.

"Z post," the commissioner said to himself in an unbelieving whisper.

The Giants hurried into a huddle, some players running onto the field while others jogged off. Troy relaxed, and the ache behind his eye now seemed almost imaginary.

"Toss sweep weak," Troy said.

The Giants lined up. The formation changed twice

before Manning took the snap and tossed the ball to his running back on a weak side sweep. The Cowboys tackled the runner for a loss. The commissioner shook his head and turned to look at Troy, blinking in disbelief.

"Again," the commissioner said.

Troy watched the screen. Only a single Giants' player ran off, a wide receiver. On came a second tight end. Troy glanced at the graphics box in the corner of the screen that told him it was second and twelve. The ball was at the Cowboys' twenty-four yard line.

"Reverse," Troy said.

He was right.

"Lead draw to the strong side," he said before the next play.

Right again, and so it went until the Giants scored and the action took a break for some commercials.

"I can't believe this," the commissioner said, his ruddy red face becoming pale and damp as he pounded his now-empty water bottle on the rich wooden table.

"I told you," Mr. Langan said to the commissioner, standing up with an enormous grin and nodding in Troy's direction.

"Honestly?" the commissioner said, shaking his head and smiling at Troy. "I wouldn't have believed it if I hadn't seen it for myself. After the Patriots scandal, we've been on the lookout for teams stealing signals, and until I saw Troy do what he does with my own eyes, I couldn't think of any other explanation."

"I told you this organization would never cheat," Mr. Langan said.

Commissioner Goodell shrugged and said, "I know it's unusual, but the truth is, he's not doing anything every coach in the NFL doesn't try to do, predict the plays the other team will run. He just does it better."

By now, Troy didn't feel a bit of the headache. Whether it was because he wasn't concentrating so hard or because the ache had actually disappeared, he didn't care.

Troy grinned at the commissioner, then turned to Seth and said, "Now we'll both be champs, me on Saturday and you and the Falcons on your way on Sunday."

"Whoa," the commissioner said, holding up a hand as his smile faded. "Don't get ahead of yourself."

"What?" Troy asked.

The commissioner tightened his jaw and inclined his head toward Seth. "He's got to get by this drug test before he gets back on the field."

"Well," Troy said with a fleeting laugh. "That's not going to be a problem."

The room went silent for a moment before Mr. Langan cleared his throat again and said, "Actually, there is a problem."

CHAPTER FORTY-SIX

SETH LOOKED DOWN AT the table and pressed his knuckles into the wood.

"No," Troy said, shaking his head and appealing to Seth. "That's not true, is it, Seth? There's no way you failed that drug test."

"It's not that he failed the test," Mr. Langan said, looking at the commissioner, who wore a serious scowl. "It's that he didn't pass it."

"What does that mean?" Troy's mom asked.

"It means just that," Mr. Langan said, turning to her. "They had a problem at the lab. It happens sometimes. We tried to have it rushed through and the samples got contaminated."

"So, you can do another, right?" Troy asked.

"Of course," Mr. Langan said.

"But we won't get the results until Monday," the commissioner said. "So there's no way I can let Seth play on Sunday."

Seth's head dropped until his chin bumped his chest, and he squeezed the top of his nose between a finger and a thumb as he shook his head.

"It's just one game, Seth," the commissioner said.

"But we're in the hunt for the playoffs," Seth said, "and *I'm* the one who works with Troy. One game can make all the difference this late in the season, for the team, and for my career, too. And I'm also thinking about another game, a game on Saturday."

"Saturday?" Mr. Langan said.

"I'm supposed to coach Troy's team in the Junior League Football state championship," Seth said, giving Troy a pained look. "If I'm not cleared, I can't coach. I made a deal with the league president and the parents."

"But that's not fair," Troy said, panic filling him at the thought of Mr. Renfro as their coach. "There *has* to be a way Seth can prove he's telling the truth."

The commissioner shook his head, and Mr. Langan said, "There's no way without the test. The only thing I can think of is if you could prove that doctor is lying."

"That would do it," the commissioner said, "but I don't see that happening, and anything short of that won't be good enough. After the halftime interview on *Monday Night Football*, the entire country is talking about this—not just sports fans, but school kids, teachers, cabdrivers. Seth Halloway is a name everyone recognizes and, until this, it was a name people associated with everything good in sports. This is a huge black eye for the league, and it won't go away easily."

"We've got to *make* him tell the truth," Troy said.

The grown-ups just stared at him.

"I mean, Gumble is *lying*," Troy said, his voice losing steam. "I know he is."

Mr. Langan cleared his throat and said, "But we'll have to prove that he is."

Troy looked at his mom. She pressed her lips tight together and nodded her head, then said, "Meantime, you've got school tomorrow, Troy."

They said goodbye to the owner and the commissioner. When they got outside, Seth suggested that Troy ride home with his mom.

"Not that I don't want you with me, buddy," Seth said, "but why don't you give your mom some company?"

Troy rode with his mom for a minute in silence before she said, "So, you ready for this?"

"The championship game?" Troy asked.

"Not that," his mom said. "The media frenzy."

"What frenzy?"

"Troy, you don't just predict plays for an NFL team, cause a scandal on national television, then get cleared by the commissioner himself without creating a media frenzy, a storm," his mom said. "You thought they wanted to interview you before? They won't be asking now. They'll be parking their trucks at the end of the driveway."

"But there's no scandal," Troy said. "Commissioner Goodell said it's okay. I just do what every coach in the NFL tries to do, only better."

"Troy, no one has ever done what you can do," his mom said. "People are going to want to talk to you about it. The scandal is people thinking the team is cheating, and Seth is cheating. Even if it's not true, it's a scandal."

"But if I'm on TV, people can see that I'm telling the truth. They can hear our side of it. It'll be good," Troy said, unable to contain the excitement creeping into the distress he felt over Seth's situation.

This would be his first taste of real fame. Everyone—including the father he never knew—would see him, Troy White, talking about his gift on national TV. They would see, and they wouldn't be able to help but admire him.

"Of course, some of it will be good," his mom said, "but sometimes it's hard."

"What could be hard about sitting there talking to Larry King?" Troy asked.

His mom glanced at him, sighed, and said, "I guess you'll just have to find out. I don't see any other way around it."

That made sense to Troy, and he was too excited

about the possibilities to worry about the concern in his mom's voice. When they got home, she told him he'd better get to sleep. Exhausted, Troy crawled into bed, trying to come up with a way they could save Seth as their coach, and fell asleep quicker than if he'd been hit by a brick.

CHAPTER FORTY-SEVEN

SETH DROPPED TROY OFF at school Friday morning, and Troy quickly found Nathan and Tate at Tate's locker.

Before he could tell them anything, Jamie Renfro sauntered past with a couple of his goons and said, "Hey, White, I saw in the paper your mom's boyfriend didn't pass his drug test. Gee, what a surprise. I hope you're ready to ride the bench in that championship game."

Renfro and his buddies laughed together before Renfro said, "'Cause you know my dad's a much better judge of talent than that juice monster who's smooching with your mom."

"Yeah, you're dad's amazing," Tate said. "For a quitter."

"I wish you were a guy," Jamie said, his face turning

purple with anger. "I'd smash your face."

Nathan glowered at Jamie and balled his fists. "Lucky for you she's not, then."

Jamie tried to grin, but instead he glanced at Nathan's snarling face, cleared his throat, and walked away with his goons.

"Is it true?" Nathan asked after they'd gone. "Seth might not be our coach?"

"Looks like he can't," Troy said, and he told them what had happened.

They stood for a minute, looking at one another in silence.

"It's bad for us," Troy said, "but it's bad for Seth, too."

"It's a lot worse for us," Nathan said. "If Seth gets cleared, he'll be back next week. This is our only chance."

"Yeah, but you know what they say NFL stands for, don't you?" Troy asked him.

"National Football League," Nathan said, grinning and puffing out his chest.

"Yeah, but also Not for Long," Troy said. "As in, your career is over before you know it. Anything that speeds up your departure you avoid like the plague."

"How does this speed up Seth's departure from football?" Nathan asked.

"If Troy's sending plays in through the defensive coordinator," Tate said, "Seth's backup is going to be making plays all over the field."

"He's younger than Seth," Troy said, "and faster, too."

"He doesn't hit harder than Seth," Tate said, her dark eyes sparkling.

"But did you see when they printed the players' salaries in the newspaper? He makes about a third of the money Seth does," Troy said. "And if he plays as well, I don't care how much they like Seth, football is a business, and businesses cut costs whenever they can."

Wearing a pained expression, Tate said, "There's gotta be a way to prove Gumble and Peele are liars, for us *and* for Seth."

"What we should do is string that dope Gumble up by his feet and stuff chili peppers up his nose," Nathan said.

Tate made a face of disgust and asked, "What?"

"Hey, I saw it in a movie," Nathan said.

"I kept thinking about it last night," Troy said. "There's nothing we can do."

"Don't say 'nothing,'" Tate said.

"Tell me you're not actually saying we can string him up," Troy said.

"No," Tate said, shaking her head, "not peppers up the nose."

The bell rang and they began to move toward their different homerooms.

"Then what?" Troy asked.

"We trick him," Tate said, stopping to face them.

"Who?" Nathan said, wrinkling his brow. "Seth?"

"No," Tate said with a sour face, "Gumble. We trick him into admitting he lied."

"How?" Troy asked.

Troy's homeroom teacher appeared in the doorway, glared at the three of them, and tapped his watch before pointing his finger inside the classroom.

"Let's go, boys. Miss McGreer," he said, "you better get going to your homeroom, too, young lady. You're late."

"Don't worry about how," Tate said as she hurried past the teacher. "I've got a doctor's appointment, so I won't see you in lunch, but you two just meet me after school. And bring your bikes."

CHAPTER FORTY-EIGHT

TROY KNEW THAT ANY plan Tate thought up would be a good one, and in his excitement he forgot about the plague of reporters his mom predicted would be waiting outside their house. When the bus approached the dirt-road turnoff on Route 141, the driver had to veer away from the edge of the road to avoid the white television vans lined up along the gravel shoulder.

"What in tarnation?" the driver said aloud, locking his eyes on Troy in the big rearview mirror above his head.

Troy shrugged and got up from his seat, moving down the aisle and avoiding eye contact with the kids, trying to ignore the ones with their faces pressed to the windows and the murmurs of excitement. Troy heard his name being whispered in the undercurrent of voices, and it made the blood rush to his face. A crowd of reporters surged toward the bus door, calling his name. Camera- and sound men followed close behind.

"Is it true? Are you a football genius?" one of the reporters shouted, pushing a microphone into Troy's face as he stepped off the bus.

"I guess," Troy said, cameras going off.

The adults clamored and pushed one another so that their questions, pitched like hard rain on a tin roof, became confusing. Amid the noise, the sudden blast from a car horn made everyone look. There in the dirt drive, behind the windshield of the green Bug, Troy's mom waved frantically to him. Troy ducked under the cameras and dodged through the crowd, slipping into the VW and slamming shut the door.

His mom popped the car into reverse, and the motor whined as they flew backward down the dirt track, leaving a cloud of glimmering dust in their wake.

"What the heck was that?" Troy said, his mouth still hanging open.

"A frenzy," his mom said.

"Will they follow us?" he asked.

"I already told them that the first one to set foot on our property I'd have arrested," she said. "They just got here or I would have picked you up from school. I called, but the buses had already left."

"Man, that was crazy," Troy said as they pulled to a stop in the middle of the red patch of clay.

His mom only nodded her head.

"But they won't come down here?" Troy asked, peering up the dirt drive.

"No," she said, getting out of the car, "but I think we're going to have to pick one show and do an interview, an exclusive, or else they won't leave us alone."

"If we pick one, what will all the others do?" Troy asked, following her up the steps and into the house.

His mom plunked herself down at the kitchen table and said, "Once the first interview airs, the other shows will take little segments of it and do their own stories. Once that happens, they'll stop pestering us. It's a race to be first, and once you do the first interview, the race is over. Do you understand?"

"I guess," Troy said, thinking of the wasted opportunities if he appeared on just one show but trusting his mom. He knew how hard she'd worked over the past couple of years to get her master's degree in public relations, with straight As. "So, who are we going to talk to? Larry King? I love Larry King."

"Let me go through the messages," she said, standing up and heading for her bedroom, where she kept her desk and computer. "Cecilia Fetters e-mailed me a bunch of requests that came in through the team. I'll make some calls and figure this thing out. We can talk about it tonight at dinner. Seth's coming over."

Seth's name reminded him of Tate and her idea.

"Can I ride my bike?" Troy asked after a moment,

raising his voice so she could hear him from the bedroom.

His mom popped her head around the corner. "Are you crazy? You can't go back down there."

"Not there," Troy said. "To Tate's. I'll take the trail through the pines. They'll never see me."

His mom wrinkled her face but said, "Well, okay, but you stay away from that pack of hyenas, right?"

"Of course," Troy said.

When his mom disappeared, Troy hurried outside. From the shed, he removed his most prized possession, the twelve-speed mountain bike his mom gave him on his last birthday. For a Falcons fan as devoted as Troy, the red frame and black trim couldn't be more perfect.

He mounted the machine and started off down the driveway. He reached the path through the pines, relishing the smooth action of the pedals and the soft click of the chain as he changed gears. Roots and dips in the path made the road to the Pine Grove Apartments a rough one, and the going was slow. By the time he reached the entrance to the apartment complex, Tate and Nathan were already waiting at the curb, their bikes parked in the grass.

"Where you been?" Nathan asked.

Troy explained the media frenzy to them, something they'd missed since the bus dropped them off before Troy's stop.

"You should do an interview with Howie Long,"

Nathan said. "My dad likes his truck commercials."

"No, Robin Roberts," Tate said. "She's an athlete *and* a real journalist."

"Howie Long's as real as it gets, sister," Nathan said.

Tate rolled her eyes.

"Don't worry about it," Troy said. "My mom will figure that all out. Anyway, what's the deal, Tate? What's the plan?"

CHAPTER FORTY-NINE

"THIS," NATHAN SAID, SLINGING a backpack off his shoulders and removing a video camera. "Tate thought her dad had one of those Dictaphones, but we couldn't find it. We thought the whole thing was a bust, but then I said, 'Hey, what about a video camera,' and she said—"

"Great idea," Tate said, beaming at Nathan.

Nathan grinned and nodded proudly.

"What are you two talking about?" Troy asked.

"I made an appointment with Gumble," Tate said.

"Why?" Troy asked, tightening his grip on the handlebars of his bike.

"To make sure he'd be at his place," Tate said. "But instead of me, you walk in and start grilling him."

"Grilling?" Troy said.

"You know," Tate said, "'Hey, Gumble, you think you

can get away with this? You know you're lying.' That kind of stuff."

"And I'm supposed to videotape him answering me?" Troy asked. "Like, 'Hey, Gumble, you don't mind if I tape this for national TV, do you?'"

"The camera stays in the backpack," Tate said. "We turn it on before he goes in."

"You won't see it, but it'll record your voices," Nathan said, "and we'll be able to *hear* it."

Troy studied them for a minute, then said, "Okay. I get it. But the whole thing with this camera in the bag while I grill him? I don't know. What if he gets suspicious?"

"Maybe we could wait outside the door and record what he says from there?" Nathan said.

Troy chewed on his lower lip. "The door's too thick, I think."

"Come on," Tate said. "We can talk on our way. The appointment is for four. We've got to ride."

They mounted their bikes and set off down the road, keeping to the shoulder and taking a back route where the traffic wasn't as heavy. As Troy rode, his mind began to twist with discomfort at the thought of just walking in and grilling Gumble. By the time they cruised into the shopping center where Gumble's office was, Troy felt ready to throw up.

They rode their bikes around back, past the big green Dumpsters used by Fantastic Fitness and over a sea of broken glass, cigarette butts, and crushed beer cans. At the far corner, they stopped next to another pair of Dumpsters, and a foul smell wafted down at them. They got off their bikes anyway. Tate peered around the corner of the brick building.

"That must be where he keeps his car," she said.

Troy looked and saw a small BMW convertible next to an unmarked metal door halfway toward the front of the building. Tate held her backpack out to Troy. He took the pack while Tate removed the camera, switched it on, and activating the recorder, then zipped it back up inside. His heart began to race at the thought of Gumble's cold, knowing eyes looking right through the backpack and seeing the recorder.

"Get going," she said. "There's only twenty minutes on the tape."

Troy shouldered the pack, took a step around the corner, then stopped.

"Wait," he said, shedding the backpack and switching off the recorder.

"It's four o'clock now," Tate said, looking at her watch. "You have to go."

"I just don't think I can walk in there with this thing and start asking questions without him wondering what's in the bag," Troy said.

"What are you, scared?" Nathan asked.

"No. I'm nervous," Troy said. "This guy gives me the creeps. His eyes. It's like he can see what you're thinking. We're only going to get one shot at this, and I just don't want to blow it."

"Just keep cool," Nathan said. "He won't notice."

"But if he can't keep cool," Tate said, "there's no sense pretending he can."

Then an idea popped into Troy's head. He snapped his fingers and said, "I got it. Keep cool. Yes. We *can* do this."

CHAPTER FIFTY

"YOU CAN KEEP COOL?" Tate asked.

"No, but when I went into Gumble's office with Seth, it was freezing in there," Troy said. "The guy wears a sweater, it's so cold."

"What are you saying?" Nathan asked. "You can keep cool or you can't. It's cold in there. The buzzing in your brain must be back pretty bad."

"My brain's fine. It's cold because of these huge AC vents," Troy said. "They take the air through the whole building, so they're huge. The one in Gumble's office is big enough for a kid to fit in. The vent is right over his desk. You guys could take the camera and get up in there and get the whole thing with Gumble, both audio and video. He'll never know."

"We can't just get into the vent," Tate said, puckering her lips.

Troy looked up at the roof and took a couple steps back. He pointed to the Dumpster.

"Why not? We could climb up on top of the Dumpster and I could help boost you guys up," Troy said. "Gumble's office is in the back corner of the building, almost right under that unit."

"But we can't just crawl inside the AC vent," Tate said.

"Actually," Nathan said, staring up at it and narrowing his eyes, "we could."

CHAPTER FIFTY-ONE

"WE COULD?" TATE ASKED.

Nathan looked at her and nodded.

"Yeah?" Tate said, raising one eyebrow. "Okay, Einstein, how?"

"My dad works for We Cool It," Nathan said.

"So?" Tate said, stamping her foot impatiently.

"You remember when we did that Take Your Children to Work Day thing at school, where we had to go with our mom or dad and write a report on what they do?" Nathan asked.

"Sure," Tate said.

"Well," Nathan said, "me and my dad spent the day up on a roof like this, working on a big AC unit on the blink. One of the things they thought it might have been was all this sheetrock dust that got into the vents and was jamming up the electronics, so I had to crawl in there with my dad and clean the whole thing out."

"We don't have any tools," Tate said.

"Don't need them," Nathan said. "There should be a panel for the main duct, so you can just loosen a screw or two or even just turn a lever and you're inside. It's easy. You won't believe how big it is in there."

"It'll be dark," Tate said.

Nathan pointed to the light clamped onto the stem of his handlebars and said, "This thing comes right off. We can use it."

Troy didn't wait. He handed the backpack to Nathan, turned, and climbed up the side of the nearest Dumpster, eyeing the distance to the lip of the roof. Nathan unclipped the light from his bike and added it to the pack before pulling it on over his shoulders. Then he and Tate followed Troy until the three of them stood atop the thick metal cover.

Nathan pinched his nose. "Man, this stinks!"

"It's about to get worse," Troy said, working his fingers under the far lip of the second Dumpster's metal cover.

"Don't do that!" Nathan said as Troy raised the cover, exposing a pile of rotten filth.

Troy twisted his face and blinked at the harsh stink, wondering what could have made a smell so bad. But he balanced his feet on the edge and kept raising the lid, pushing it up hand over hand and doubling it back until it fell open. The lid clunked against the brick wall three-quarters of the way up toward the roof.

"It's like a dead skunk," Tate said, waving her hand in front of her nose and squinting her eyes from atop the first Dumpster.

"It's like pig barf," Nathan said, covering his face with both hands.

"We can use it to climb up to the roof," Troy said, peering into the open metal container and seeing a mound of broken trash bags whose spilled contents included empty cans, crushed milk cartons, old takeout boxes, baby diapers, and moldy pieces of rotten fruit, all in a soup of green slime.

Troy turned when he heard Nathan make a weird animal noise. Nathan doubled over and lost his lunch in a huge splat on the Dumpster's plate-metal cover.

"Oh my God," Tate said, pinching her nose and turning away.

"You okay?" Troy asked Nathan.

"Much better now," Nathan said, wiping the corner of his mouth with the back of his hand.

Troy shook his head and patted his hand against the metal ribbing on the underside of the second Dumpster's lid and said, "Well, come on then."

Carefully, Troy scaled the underside of the lid. When he reached the top, he wedged his toes into the narrow foothold between the lid and the brick wall and reached back to help Tate. She scrambled up like a lemur, and with Troy giving her a boost, in less than a minute she was looking back down at them from the roof.

"Aw, man," Nathan said as he begin to climb one-handed so that he could use his free hand to cover his nose.

"You'd better use two hands," Troy said, reaching down so he could grab Nathan's wrist and help pull him up.

"Uh-uh," Nathan said, shaking his head, the words garbled by his hand. "I'm not upchucking again."

"I'm telling you," Troy said.

It was at that moment Nathan's foot slipped. His eyes went wide as salad plates, and he grasped for Troy with both hands.

CHAPTER FIFTY-TWO

TROY STRAINED TO PULL Nathan up, horrified at the thought of his friend falling into the rotten mess below. By the look on his face, he could see that Nathan was even more horrified, but once Troy had him going in the right direction, Nathan scrambled up the lid as fast as Tate had.

The two of them peered down at Troy while he made his way back to the first Dumpster, carefully sidestepping Nathan's puke. Troy pinched his nose and signaled okay. Then the two of them disappeared from Troy's sight. After a couple minutes, they reappeared, both giving him a thumbs-up.

"He got it," Tate said. "He knew right where to go. And it is huge in here. Go ahead. You get in there and give it to that Gumble."

"You sure you guys are okay?" Troy asked. "The video camera, all that?"

Nathan reached over his shoulder and patted the backpack. "We're cool."

"Don't worry, we'll be right there," Tate said. "But get going now. The stink from that Dumpster is pretty bad up here, and I think it's only a matter of time before it's going to get into the vents."

"You got it," Troy said, sounding a lot more confident than he felt.

His two friends disappeared and Troy climbed down, glad to be away from the stench of the Dumpsters but wishing he could trade places with them, safe up in the vent while he'd be face-to-face with a guy he knew must be evil to the bone. He walked along the building, past the BMW, and around the front corner to the mostly empty storefronts of the brand-new shopping center.

As he reached for the glass door in the front of Gumble's office, a heavy middle-aged woman on crutches appeared, struggling through the inner door. She wore no cast on her leg, but her face was twisted in pain.

"Thank you, honey," she said as Troy held the outer door for her. "You're a gentleman."

"You're welcome," Troy said. "Uh, did you hear anything in the AC vent when you were in there?"

The woman looked at him as if he'd asked her if she'd like to take a trip to the moon.

"No," she said, drawing the word out long and low.

"Thanks," Troy said, and headed inside. He walked carefully down the long hallway, put his ear to the door, and listened for a minute before taking one final deep breath and walking into Gumble's office.

Gumble stood over a long box covering the top of his desk, packing away his skeleton. He wore the same lab coat, but this time with a red cardigan sweater over his crisp white T-shirt. His face looked even more like the color of a carrot than Troy remembered. The bleached-blond hair on his head contrasted sharply with the brown filaments sprouting from his neck and arms. After tucking the left arm of the skeleton into the box, Gumble looked up.

He stared for a minute with his cold blue eyes, processing who Troy was, before he pointed a finger and asked, "What are *you* doing here?"

CHAPTER FIFTY-THREE

TROY'S EYES DARTED TO the air vent above Gumble's desk. He could see nothing behind the grate except empty blackness until he moved his head to one side and spotted the tiny power light from the video camera. Troy knew it was showtime.

"I want to know why you lied about Seth," Troy said, stepping toward the desk and pointing right back at the shady doctor. "Seth never used steroids!"

"Where is Seth?" Gumble asked, his eyes searching the doorway behind Troy.

"Not here," Troy said. "You're ruining his career and I want to know why."

"You got a brass bottom, you know that, kid?" Gumble said, returning his glare to Troy. "Who do you think you are, barging in here like this? I got an appointment coming in."

"That was my friend who called you," Troy said, folding his arms across his chest. "I'm your appointment."

"I ought to send your mother a bill for this," Gumble said. "You know that?"

"You ought to tell the truth is what you ought to do."

"What's it to you?"

"Seth is a good person," Troy said. "He never did anything wrong except trust you. So you did lie, didn't you?"

Gumble looked around and snorted. "Yeah, I lied. So what? You see this?"

Gumble wagged his head around, and Troy saw the skeleton wasn't the only thing that had been boxed up.

"Seth Halloway isn't the only one in hot water," Gumble said. "It wasn't my idea to smear him with dirt, but Peele gave me time to get out of town if I went along with it."

Troy gave him a puzzled look.

"I'm out of here, kid," Gumble said. "Peele dug a little too deep into my past, found out I lost my license back in Ohio, then Nevada, before I came here."

"You're not even a doctor?" Troy said.

"Sure I am, kid," Gumble said with a crooked smile. "Once a doctor, always a doctor. So I bought myself a free pass by turning Seth in for juicing."

"Juicing?" Troy said.

"Steroids."

"But you didn't give him steroids," Troy said.

Gumble rolled his hands over, palms up, fingers splayed out wide. "I'm sure he did them sometime, kid. What's the difference if I say he did them now?"

"You don't know that," Troy said.

"A lot of professional athletes do," Gumble said.

"Well, Seth doesn't and never has, except for an injury," Troy said. "You lied."

"Well, too bad for him," Gumble said. "What can I say? Crap happens, kid. You'll learn."

"Peele asked you to lie?" Troy said. "That's what you're saying?"

"Of course he did," Gumble said. "He made me lie. I got nothing against Seth Halloway, kid, but it's every man for himself. Halloway's got more money than Bill Gates, playing in the NFL all these years. He's near the end, anyway. He doesn't need it, but I do. I can't afford any more trouble following me around like a dog. I'm sorry, kid. I'm not a bad guy."

"Oh yes you are," Troy said.

A distant banging noise sounded in the vent. Troy thought of his friends, but the sudden blast of air-conditioning told him the noise had come from the AC unit itself. But what came out of the vent next was worse than a noise.

Gumble froze and sniffed the air before crumpling his face.

"What the heck is that smell?" Gumble said, and turned to stare up at the vent, where the light on Nathan's camera glowed like the red eye of a small rodent.

CHAPTER FIFTY-FOUR

GUMBLE CAST A QUICK, hateful look at Troy, then shoved the skeleton box so that it tipped and spilled its contents out onto the floor. The skull rolled to a stop at Troy's feet, grinning up at him with empty eye sockets. Gumble stepped up on his chair and then onto the desk so he could peer directly into the vent.

With one hand pinching his nose, Gumble stabbed a finger at the vent and shouted, "You little balls of crap! I see what you're at! I'll get you!"

Troy stood frozen as Gumble jumped down off the desk and leaped across the room, throwing open the door and disappearing out into the hallway. Troy heard the side door bang open as Gumble sprinted outside, heading for the Dumpsters in back.

"Troy!" Tate shouted. "Oh my God! Is he coming?"

“Yes,” Troy said, the word coming out as a croak.

“Get me out of here!” Nathan shouted.

“Can he get in the vent?” Troy asked, suddenly alert, the whole picture of what was happening clear to him now.

“Yes,” Tate said, “it’s open and the trapdoor is huge.”

Troy darted to the desk, tossing the chair out from behind it and kicking the bones out of his way. He put his shoulder to it. With all his strength, he began to push. Slowly the desk went. He shoved at it until it bumped into the wall, then hopped up on top of it so that he was staring into the frightened faces of Nathan and Tate.

“Hurry!” Tate said. “I think I hear him!”

Troy gripped the edges of the grate and tried to pull.

“Kick it!” Troy shouted.

“We can’t turn around!” Nathan yelled back, but he wormed his way past Tate and began to bang on the grate from the inside with a fist, bowing it out.

Troy saw the two thick screws holding it firm and cast his eyes back around the room. A screwdriver lay on the floor next to the skeleton’s metal stand. Troy jumped down, snatched it, and leaped back up, attacking the screws with the tool.

“Stop banging it,” Troy said.

“I’m not!” Nathan said.

"Then what's that sound?" Troy asked, working frantically, the blade of the screwdriver slipping and gouging the wall.

Troy held still.

BANG. BANG. BANG.

The hollow sound echoed through the vent.

"It's him!" Tate screamed. "Troy! Help us!"

Troy attacked the screw again, his hand shaking so hard he had to steady it with the other.

"Hurry!" Nathan shouted.

BANG. BANG. BANG.

The sound kept getting closer.

The first screw came free.

BANG. BANG. Louder and louder, the sounds came quicker as Gumble increased the speed of his crawl.

Troy attacked the second screw.

BANG. BANG.

It sounded like Gumble was nearly on top of them, and Troy heard the phony doctor cackle in an evil way. He turned the screw once, twice, then grabbed the grate and yanked with all his might, swinging it aside.

Tate shot out like an otter. Troy caught her and dumped her down on the desk. Nathan scrabbled out from behind, his head, shoulders, and arms free. He tossed his camera to Tate before he froze and his face went white.

Something sucked him back into the vent.

"Ahhhh!" Nathan screamed, kicking.

In the dark hole of the vent, beyond Nathan's wide-eyed, screaming face and thrashing legs, Troy could see the crazed smile and the hairy spider-arms of Doc Gumble gripping Nathan's ankles.

CHAPTER FIFTY-FIVE

NATHAN COILED HIS FREE LEG, and with a wild cry he let fly with a kick that would have made Chuck Norris proud. His heel connected with Gumble's nose. A popping sound exploded through the vent, and Nathan's foot came away from Gumble's face, spattered in blood.

Nathan slithered free, then shot out of the vent just as Tate had, only when Troy tried to catch him, they both collapsed on the desk, then rolled off onto the floor amid the rattle of loose bones.

"Get up!" Tate shouted, tugging at them.

They scrambled to their feet and bolted out the office door. Troy guided them down a short hall that led to the side door, and they burst outside in front of the BMW, dashed around the corner, and grabbed their bikes.

Troy sensed Gumble above them and looked up to

see the phony doctor's bloody face, snarling at them as he swung his legs over the side of the roof. Troy, Nathan, and Tate started running with their bikes, wheeling to speed them up so they could jump on and keep going. Almost as one they swung their legs up and over their seats. Nathan was off fast, but Tate—trying to do the whole operation with the video camera still in hand—slipped and went crashing to the pavement. When Gumble's feet hit the lip of the Dumpster's open lid, he spun, bracing his hands against the brick wall, and leered at Tate's fallen bike.

Tate lay on her back beneath the bike, extending the camera up in the air to show Troy she hadn't let it break.

Gumble laughed and launched himself toward the closed top of the first Dumpster. Troy gasped. Gumble would jump down on Tate before she could get up.

But if Tate was going down, Troy was going with her.

CHAPTER FIFTY-SIX

WHEN GUMBLE'S FEET HIT the top of the Dumpster, they landed in the pool of Nathan's barf. Instead of coming to a stop, his feet flew up to the sky, right out from under him. Gumble's arms made pinwheels in the air, but he never had a chance. Backward he fell, right into the open Dumpster, with a sickening squish. Gumble howled and thrashed, trying to get out.

Skidding to a sideways stop, Troy raced to Tate's side, then jumped off his bike to help her up and steady her.

"You okay?" he asked, raising his voice above Gumble's wailing fury and disgust.

Tate grinned at him, holding up the camera, and said, "I'm fine, and so is this. Come on."

They started off and got halfway along the length of

the shopping center before they heard Gumble shouting at them from the Dumpster.

"You come back here!" he screamed. "Get back here, I said!"

Troy shot a glance over his shoulder, grinning at the slimed-over form of the fake doctor. Gumble's white lab coat showed off the brown, yellow, and green filth from the Dumpster like an artist's blank canvas. A used diaper clung to his shoulder, and a glop of something rotten rested in his spiky hair like some foul bird in its nest.

"See you on TV, Gumble!" Troy hollered, giggling to himself at how much Gumble reminded him of Peele when Seth had dumped him upside down into the trash can.

Tate waved the camera up over her head and gave a war cry as they rounded the far corner of the shopping center and surged across the parking lot toward home.

CHAPTER FIFTY-SEVEN

THEY DIDN'T CATCH UP to Nathan until they got to the Pine Grove Apartments.

"Where'd you guys go? Sheesh," Nathan said. "Man, I never looked back until I got here and I'm like, 'What the heck happened?'"

"Tate fell. She almost got caught," Troy said. "Nice going on Gumble's nose."

"Hey, you think Tate's the only kicker? How about me kicking that goofball?" Nathan said. "He messed with the wrong mule."

"He also slipped in your barf," Troy said, his lip curling with disgust.

"Otherwise, he would have had me," Tate said.

"Strategic barfing is another one of my many strengths," Nathan said, beaming.

"Hey, let's see what you guys got," Troy said, reaching for the camera.

They played back the video and heard everything they needed. Nathan snuck the camera into the back door of his family's apartment, and Tate headed in for dinner, too, telling Troy she'd see him at practice. Troy took the mini-DVD and stuffed it into his pocket before setting off on his bike toward the path through the pines. Seth's H2 sat in the dirt patch, next to his mom's VW Bug. When Troy went inside, his mom was at the stove and Seth sat at the kitchen table going over the clipboard he used for the Duluth Tigers' game plan.

"Hey," Seth said, looking as glum as he sounded.

"Hey, hey," Troy said, pulling the disc out of his pocket and holding it up like a gold coin. "Look at this."

"What have you got?" Seth asked.

"Your ticket to coaching us in the state championship," Troy said, handing it to Seth with an enormous grin, "and playing on Sunday, too."

"What?" Seth said, turning it over in his hand.

"What Roger Goodell said he needed," Troy said, "and the proof to show Mr. Flee you're not the liar, Peele is. I got Gumble on tape, admitting he lied. Peele threatened to turn him in. Something about him not having his doctor's license."

Troy's mom dropped a spoon into the sink and asked, "What did you do?"

"Nothing," Troy said. "We tricked him."

"How?" Seth asked.

Troy told them the story, leaving out the part about Gumble chasing them, because he didn't want to worry his mom.

"You sure it's on there?" Seth asked.

"We watched it," Troy said, nodding his head. "Whoever does my interview, maybe they can show this on national TV. What do you think? That'll clear Seth's name for good."

Seth smiled and said, "I like the way you're thinking."

Troy smiled back proudly.

"But I want to show this to Flee myself," Seth said, holding up the disc, "so there's no confusion about tomorrow night and me coaching the team. Once Flee sees it, he can let Mr. Renfro know *he's* the one who'll be riding the bench for the championship game. Then I'll show Mr. Langan and he can get a copy of it to the commissioner. I got to believe Goodell will have me back in the lineup Sunday and we can keep this playoff run alive."

"What about your knees?" Troy's mom asked.

Seth shrugged. "A little more ice, a little more ibuprofen. Maybe drain them out with a needle and pump a little cortisone in. I've done it before."

Troy and his mom grimaced together.

"I've said it before," Seth said, looking at them, "it's a rough way to make a living, but it's what I do."

"Is it all really worth it?" Troy's mom asked.

"Yes," Seth said, "especially when you're in the hunt for a championship. How many people get to do that?"

Troy nodded, thinking of his own championship the very next day, and said, "Not many."

"Right," Seth said, "not many get to go for what you're going for tomorrow night, either."

"I was just thinking that," Troy said.

"I bet," Seth said. "So let's eat and go have a short practice to tune up, then get a good night's sleep before the big game. I'll call Mr. Langan and bring this disc in tomorrow after I show it to Flee."

"What about the interview?" Troy asked.

"You want to do Larry King?" his mom asked.

"Yeah," Troy said, his breath going out of him.

"Then we're on at nine tonight," she said, reaching for the phone. "I wanted to check with you before I made it official. We'll head down to CNN Center after your practice."

"Will he be there?" Troy asked.

"No, he's in Los Angeles," she said. "We'll do an uplink."

"A what?"

"A satellite hookup," she said. "We'll be in a studio here, talking to him live. The picture gets sent up on a satellite and down to his studio, so it's like we're right there."

"Oh," Troy said, "I thought I'd get to meet him."

"You'll meet him," she said. "Just not in person. Not

in person tonight, anyway."

"You mean maybe another time?" Troy asked.

His mom looked at Seth and said, "If this thing goes the way I think it will, there will be other opportunities."

"What's that mean?" Troy asked.

His mom walked over to him and put a hand on his shoulder, giving it a squeeze.

"Whether we like it or not," she said, "this thing is going to make you somewhat famous, Troy. It's going to change our lives."

Troy studied her face, the swirl of doubt in her eyes, the hint of a frown, and asked, "You mean in a *good* way, right?"

CHAPTER FIFTY-EIGHT

"MOSTLY GOOD," TROY'S MOM said, forcing a weak smile. "But some isn't going to be so good."

"Why?" Troy asked.

"When people know who you are," Seth said, "it's like turning your life into a billboard on the side of a road. Most people pass by and they recognize you and think it's pretty neat. They might stop and take a picture next to you, or just wave and beep their horn. But every once in a while, you get some goofball who's going to throw a rotten piece of fruit or a broken bottle at you, just because."

"Just because?" Troy said.

"Because they don't like that you're up there on a billboard and they're not," his mom said. "It's part of it."

"Even if you're nice to everyone?" Troy asked.

"Yes," his mom said, "even if you're nice. I don't want you to think it's *all* fun, Troy. Some of it's going to hurt."

"Like football," Seth said. "It's fun, but it can hurt. It's worth it, though. Because of the fun part."

Troy smiled at him and nodded. "I thought that."

"Okay," his mom said, glancing at the clock and turning back to the stove, "time to eat, then practice, then you become famous."

After dinner, Troy changed into his practice gear. His mom packed him some clothes to wear for Larry King, and they drove off down the dirt driveway together. The reporters still waited with their TV trucks, but Seth drove right through them, kicking up a cloud of dust.

"How long will they stay?" Troy asked, looking over the back of the seat.

"They'll be gone after the word spreads that you're doing *Larry King Live*," his mom said.

"Good," Troy said.

"Thought you said you were ready to be famous," Seth said, glancing at him in the rearview mirror with a mischievous grin.

Practice ran like a Swiss watch, with everyone going to the right place at the right time. Pass patterns were crisp. Troy's passes were precise. Handoffs went smoothly. On defense, with Troy reading the offense and calling signals, the Tigers were able to swarm to the ball like angry hornets. By the time Seth called them all together, he was wearing a giant smile.

"Good," he said. "Very good. Play like this tomorrow night and you'll all walk away champions."

CHAPTER FIFTY-NINE

TROY MARVELED AT HOW many people it took to run a TV studio. There were wires and monitors and desks everywhere, and people darted in and out all over the place with headsets and clipboards. He was taken down a hallway and into a white room filled with mirrors and lights and several barber chairs.

"Makeup," his mom explained.

"For what?" Troy asked.

"You."

Troy raised an eyebrow.

"It's okay," Seth said. "Welcome to TV. Everyone does it."

"Man," Troy said, shaking his head and hoping Nathan wouldn't hear about it.

Someone sat him down in one chair and his mom in

another, since Larry King had asked that she be with him during the interview. Troy tried to stay still while one woman put makeup on his face and another messed around with his hair. A third patted his dark blue polo shirt with a piece of tape to remove the lint. Troy's mom smirked at him.

"Part of what being famous is all about," she said, winking at him in the mirror from her own chair.

"Man," Troy said again, still shaking his head.

A young man led them halfway back down the hall and into a smaller room with a desk and chair facing two cameras. Behind it, the wall had been plastered with a photo of downtown Atlanta.

"We could be in Alaska for all everyone knows," Troy said.

He and his mom sat behind the desk and two other people attached microphones to their collars, running the thin black cables up the backs of their shirts before plugging earbuds into their ears so they could hear Larry. A woman who said she was the stage manager told them they'd be able to see Larry on a TV monitor that she wheeled over to the side of the room.

"But don't look at that when you're talking," she told Troy and his mom. "Just look right at the camera."

His mom nodded. Troy gripped the edge of the desk, and his hands began to sweat. A different woman appeared from nowhere and set two bottles of water in front of them. Troy's hands shook as he cracked the cap. He gulped down some water to try to wet his dry mouth.

Before he knew it, Troy was hearing Larry King in his earbud. Troy mumbled hello to the booming but friendly voice, then listened to his mom talk as if she'd known Larry for years.

"You okay, Troy?" Larry asked.

"Yes," Troy said, swallowing.

"Great," Larry said, "we've got about four minutes, then I'll be back with you."

Troy's earbud went quiet. Seth gave him a thumbs-up.

"Break a leg," Seth said, then ducked out of the studio.

Troy looked at his mom. She reached for his hand and gave it a squeeze. He blinked at the spotlights and shielded his eyes.

"You okay?" his mom asked.

Troy nodded, wondering if, when Larry came back live and they were on TV across the entire world, he'd even be able to speak.

A sudden flurry of talking erupted in his earpiece. People began counting down, music blared, and Larry King's voice boomed, welcoming everyone to his show.

"And tonight," Larry said, "from CNN Center in Atlanta with his mom, Tessa, a boy whose mental abilities some say will change the balance of power in the NFL—a boy so extraordinarily brilliant that league commissioner Roger Goodell, who'll join us later from New York, at first suspected the Atlanta Falcons of a cheating scheme more elaborate than the New England Patriots infamous Spygate scandal. But that was before Goodell met and witnessed firsthand what this football genius can do. Troy White . . ."

Three red lights above the camera's lens burned suddenly out at Troy while Larry kept talking.

Troy took a deep breath and heard Larry King say his name again, this time waiting for him to say something back.

CHAPTER SIXTY

THE TOWERING BANK OF LIGHTS glared down onto the pristine grass field, muscling back the black of the night sky beyond. The concrete bowl of the Georgia Tech stadium seemed twenty stories high, and already several thousand fans filled the best seats.

"Man," Nathan said, buckling his chinstrap, "I thought you were gonna choke on your tongue. Like a seizure or something."

"Thanks a lot," Troy said, scowling and putting his own helmet on.

"Your head's not still buzzing, is it?" Nathan asked with a serious face.

"No," Troy said, frowning. "My head feels fine. I looked that bad?"

"No. No one even noticed," Tate said, tightening the belt on her football pants. "After that first—I don't know, hiccup—you did great. You *sounded* like a football genius, and that Larry King is so nice."

"Speaking of Larry King, it's time for me to make my own TV debut," Nathan said, pointing up at the press box, where cameras with Georgia Cable System stickers on their sides poked their noses down at the field. "When I score tonight, I got a dance that'll make the highlights on ESPN."

"How are you going to score?" Tate asked. "You're a lineman."

"Defense, my friend," Nathan said, wagging his hips and throwing out a stiff arm. "You gotta visualize it to make it happen, and I see myself scooping up a fumble and going on a rumble."

Tate shook her head and snorted.

"Hey, you gotta have a dream, Tate," Nathan said, dropping his hands to his sides. "As a kicker, you might not know about that."

"Forget about all that junk," Troy said. "We're a team, right? We all have to play our best tonight, every position. Let's win this thing, right? Football champs."

Troy held out a fist and Nathan and Tate pounded it with fists of their own, grunting in agreement.

When Seth blew his whistle, they jogged down under the shadow of the goalposts with the rest of the Duluth

Tigers. As they warmed up, Troy marveled at the size and speed of the Valdosta Vipers on the other end of the field, their green-and-white uniforms glowing like gems under the bright lights. Before long, cameras with stickers other than the GCS ones began to appear on the sidelines. Troy ignored them until Tate poked him in the arm.

"Did you see?" she asked. "FOX, ESPN, CBS, they're all here. Can you believe it?"

"Here for the championship?" Troy said.

"No, meathead," Tate said. "They're here to see you."

Troy looked over and saw that, in fact, the cameras were trained at him even as he spoke to Tate.

"Don't even think about them," Seth said, turning Troy and Tate around by the shoulder pads. "You've got to focus on the game. Those cameras can't do anything to help us beat Valdosta. We need all you got, Troy."

And that's what Troy gave.

The Tigers received the ball first and he set the tone, changing plays at the line of scrimmage, directing his receivers, and completing his first ten passes to score the opening touchdown. On defense, it was more of the same. While the Vipers were bigger and faster, Troy was able to predict their plays after the first four. Even though the Tigers couldn't keep Valdosta from scoring, they were able to sometimes hold them to a field goal instead of a touchdown, and twice they even made the Vipers punt. So the game went—until the fourth quarter.

That's when Troy got hurt.

CHAPTER SIXTY-ONE

TROY LAY UNDER A PILE of Valdosta defenders, gripping his throwing hand. A sort of howling noise escaped his mouth through gritted teeth. As the artificial light began to appear through the big bodies of the Vipers, so did Troy's mom and Seth.

"Let me see that," Seth said, taking Troy's right hand in his own.

Troy saw his mom's face go pale. She grimaced and looked away.

Troy forced his eyes to look.

The pointer finger on his right hand, his throwing hand, stuck out sideways from the middle joint, making an upside-down L. Seeing it made the pain worse.

"We've got to get him to the hospital," Troy's mom said.

Seth glanced at the scoreboard, then at Troy. They were ahead 35–23. Just over eleven minutes remained.

"If he goes," Seth said to Troy's mom, "we'll lose."

"You're ahead by twelve," Troy's mom said, "and he's hurt."

"We don't have to score again," Seth said, "so he won't have to throw. But if we don't have him on defense, calling the plays, this team could score forty or fifty points before it's over."

"I can't risk his health," Troy's mom said.

Seth's lower lip disappeared beneath his upper teeth. He bit down, then said, "It's dislocated. If we tape it good, it can't get any worse. I've done it plenty of times. Trust me."

"Seth," Troy's mom said with a horrified expression, "he's twelve years old. You're in the NFL."

"I want to, Mom," Troy said, blurting out his words over the searing pain.

"I can snap it back in place," Seth said, reaching for the finger.

"Oh my God," Troy's mom said. "We're talking about a junior league football game."

"I want to win, Mom," Troy said.

"He's a football player," Seth said. "This is a championship, Tessa. I've only played in a championship once in my whole life, back in high school. You always think you'll get another chance, but most people never do."

"Mom, please," Troy said. "I'm fine."

"*That's* not fine," his mom said, pointing at the dislocated finger and averting her eyes.

"It will be," Troy said. "Fix it, Seth."

Seth looked at Troy's mom. She threw her hands up in the air and began walking away.

"Fine," she said.

Seth took Troy's hand in one of his and grasped the end of his bent-over finger in the other.

"Don't look," Seth said.

CHAPTER SIXTY-TWO

TROY TRIED NOT TO make a sound, but that proved impossible. What came out, though, was a grunt worthy of an NFL player. A sweat broke out on Troy's face and he felt slightly nauseous, but when he looked down, the finger sat straight.

"Come on," Seth said, helping him off. "We'll tape it and you'll be ready for defense."

While Tate lined up to punt the ball, Seth bound Troy's pointer finger to his middle finger with thick bands of tape. Then he wrapped all four of them into one bunch and anchored the whole mess down with strips of tape that circled Troy's palm and wrist so that his arm resembled a seal's flipper more than a boy's hand. Troy took the field with the defense and did his best.

He got his players in the right position, but when it came to leading the charge and making the tackle, his hand made it tough. Not only did he feel a bolt of excruciating pain every time he hit a runner or a receiver, the tape made it much more difficult to wrap up a player and hang on. The Vipers managed to kick two field goals, closing the gap to six points.

Offense was even worse for Troy. He stayed in, telling Seth he could take the snap and hand the ball off better than his backup. He gutted it out, even though Duluth's running game never gained more than three yards on a single play. There were just fifty-three seconds left when Valdosta's halfback burst through a wave of Tigers' tacklers and into the end zone to tie the score. The extra point went through, giving Valdosta a one-point lead and setting off an explosion of cheers from the Vipers fans.

Troy jogged to the sideline with the rest of his team and gathered around Seth.

"Do *not* give up," Seth said, growling at them. "I see that look in your eyes. Well, don't do it. Don't you give up now."

Troy felt the tears welling. His words sounded choked as they came out.

"But how are we going to score?" he said. "I can't even throw a pass."

"We'll run and kick it," Seth said. "Rusty, you get us past the fifty on the kickoff. You did that once already tonight. Nathan, you and your hogs got to get us three and a half yards a carry—that's it. You've done that before, too. Now you got to do it six times in a row, get us another twenty yards, and Tate can kick a field goal to win it. She's done that before, and she'll do it again."

Everyone looked at Tate. Blood ran down from the bridge of her nose, cut after her helmet shifted from making a tackle on the last kickoff. Her eyes glittered back at them. She smiled past her mouthpiece and nodded her head.

"Bring it in," Seth said, his words now filled with an electric current that ran through them all. "We don't have to do anything we haven't done before, right? We can do this. Champs on three. One. Two. Three."

"CHAMPS!"

They broke the big huddle, and the kickoff return team took the field. Nathan lumbered to the middle of the formation and pointed at one of the Valdosta defenders, who was even bigger than he was.

"I got you, ninety-eight," Nathan said.

Troy and Tate watched, and Nathan did get number ninety-eight. Rusty also got them the ball over the fifty-yard line on his return, all the way down to the Valdosta forty-six.

"Go get them," Tate said, slapping Troy on the shoulder.

Troy jogged into the huddle and called a run play.

Three times in a row, they ran for more than three yards, giving them a first down and stopping the clock. The Tigers felt a surge of energy and confidence, but the Vipers were a great team, and the next two runs sputtered, leaving Duluth with a third down and eight yards to go. Only a pass could save them. Seth used their second-to-last time-out and ran onto the field, kneeling down in the huddle next to Troy and looking up at all of them.

"Let me try to throw it," Troy said.

Seth smiled at him but shook his head. "You can't do what you can't do. We've got to run a sweep."

"We haven't run more than three and a half yards all day," Troy said.

"Troy, you can't throw it, not a spiral," Seth said. "It's impossible. We've got to try a sweep."

"Unless," Troy said.

"Unless what?" Seth asked.

CHAPTER SIXTY-THREE

"WHAT IF I DON'T throw a spiral?" Troy said. "What if I just lob it up? Heave it like a big rock?"

"What are you talking about?" Seth asked. "It'll get intercepted and we'll lose."

"What if I throw it to someone they don't expect me to throw it to?" Troy said, pointing at Nathan.

"What'd I do?" Nathan said, touching his chest as his mouth dropped open.

"We'll show them our unbalanced formation to the right," Troy said, "only instead of having a wide receiver to the backside, we'll move all the receivers to the right side, too, and everyone will make it look like a sweep to the right. Then Nathan sneaks into the end zone and I throw it to him."

"If Nathan's the last man on the left side," Seth said, "he'll have to report in as an eligible receiver. Even though he's big and slow as a turtle, they'll cover him for sure."

"A turtle?" Nathan said, scowling.

"He doesn't have to report," Troy said, shaking his head.

"He's number ninety-nine," Seth said, pointing at Nathan's jersey. "That's not an eligible number unless you report it to the referee."

"It's not eligible in the NFL," Troy said, "but we play by high school rules, and anything between eighty and ninety-nine *is* eligible."

"You sure?" Seth said, scratching his head.

Troy nodded. "That's the rule. I know it."

"And you think you can throw it that far?" Seth asked. "Even if no one is covering him? With that finger?"

Troy set his teeth and said, "It's one pass. I can do it."

Troy said, "If we make this look like a sweep to the right, trust me, the whole defense will be running that way. Nathan can fall down like he's spastic, then sneak out to the left side and get downfield. He'll be wide open. Can we do it?"

Seth bit back a smile, nodded, and said, "Well, you're the football genius. I'm not betting against you. Nathan, think you can do it?"

"Do it?" Nathan said, his eyebrows disappearing

underneath the front pad of his helmet. "I may not be fast, but I got some slick moves. I can go spastic as good as anyone and then take this baby all the way to the house."

"Don't worry about the house," Seth said, "just get us close enough for Tate to kick a field goal. And *catch* the ball."

"With these sticky fingers?" Nathan said, holding up all ten digits, wiggling them, and splaying them wide. "How can I miss?"

Seth studied him for a second, then nodded at Troy and said, "Okay. Do it."

Seth jogged off. The ref blew the whistle and Troy called the play, repeating for his teammates exactly what each had to do, how they had to line up, and locking eyes with each player to make sure he understood. Troy broke the huddle and they jogged up to the line. Nathan looked over at Troy and winked before getting into his stance. Troy called the cadence and took the snap, wincing in pain. He pivoted the same way he would on a power sweep and took off to the right along with the rest of the Tigers. As he ran, he saw Nathan from the corner of his eye, falling to the turf before slipping back the other way.

Troy kept his hands in the position he would use if he were running a quarterback sweep, pretending the ball was tucked under his arm and covering it with his free hand. He got as far to the right as he could before he ran out of room. The Vipers' defense swarmed him. He rocked back and heaved the ball sideways in the air, sending a jolt of agony through his mangled finger. Half a second later, they knocked him to the ground.

Troy wormed his way up through the pile of bodies in time to see Nathan holding the ball high in one hand and doing a backward jig that was the silliest thing Troy had ever seen. It didn't matter, though.

Nathan was already in the end zone, under the lights.

The ref shot both hands straight up in the air.

Touchdown!

The clock on the scoreboard showed that time had run out. The game was over.

CHAPTER SIXTY-FOUR

TROY SPRINTED TO THE end zone, where he met Nathan and Tate and Seth and the entire Tigers team. They hugged one another and cheered together so loud and so hard that Troy nearly forgot about his finger. Finally, exhaustion quieted them, and the TV cameras surrounded Troy and Seth. Troy's mom appeared and let him answer questions about the game until the reporters started asking him about helping the Falcons in their playoff run.

"That's it," Troy's mom said, stepping between him and the cameras. "It's late. Troy's going to the hospital and then home."

"What about Seth?" one of the reporters shouted.

Seth shook his head and said, "Sorry, guys, I'll talk to you more tomorrow, after the game. I'm the guy driving him to the doctor's."

Troy, his mom, and Seth worked their way toward the H2 amid a clapping crowd, shaking hands with parents and football fans along the way.

A man in a suit stepped in front of them, blocking their way, and said, "Troy, I'm Doug Nash. I saw you on Larry King. I'm a lawyer and an agent. I work with some NFL players, but also the NBA, the NHL, a couple tennis players, and some TV personalities. I think I could help you get a heck of a deal with the Falcons, or even another team."

"What?" Troy said, looking at his mom for an explanation.

Troy's mom took the man's card, studied it, and said, "I'm Tessa, his mom. Thank you, I'll take your card and we'll call if we need you."

"Are you already planning on using John Marchiano, Seth's agent?" Doug Nash asked, raising his eyebrows and nodding toward Seth.

"We have no idea what we're doing," Troy's mom said. "At this point, Troy's committed to helping the Falcons."

"But not for next year, right?" Nash said. "I mean, no contract? I think I could get you one to two million dollars a year, Ms. White. Some people will say five, just to impress you, but I've made some initial inquiries and I don't like to exaggerate."

"One to two million?" Troy said, exhaling the words

like a puff of breath on a cold day. “Mom?”

“Not now, Mr. Nash,” Troy’s mom said, raising a hand. “We’ve got to get him to the doctor, and then we want to celebrate the championship. This isn’t the time or place. We’ll call you.”

They pushed past the agent and continued on toward the lighted parking lot. Seth shouted out invitations to the Tigers players and parents to spread the word that everyone was invited to his place for a postgame party. He handed his keys to Tate’s mom, asking her to get things going for him at the house and telling her that Tate knew where he kept plenty of drinks and snacks. Along the way to the truck, three other men in business suits also handed Troy their cards, asking him to call them about representing him. Troy’s mom took the cards and said they didn’t want to be bothered now.

“Mom,” Troy said as he climbed into the backseat of the H2, “are these guys serious? Can I make millions?”

His mom heaved a sigh from the front, glanced at Seth, and turned around. “Honey, let’s not think about it right now. It’s possible, yes, but let’s enjoy what you just did. Like Seth said, you don’t get to be a champion very often. Let’s just go get you checked out and then celebrate with the team.”

“I don’t really have to go to the hospital, do I, Mom?” Troy asked. “I’ll miss the party.”

“I bet I can get Doc Garrett to take a picture at his

clinic. It's on the way home," Seth said, starting up the truck. "Just to make sure it's not broken."

"This late at night?" Troy's mom said.

"He'll do it for me," Seth said.

Seth took out his cell phone and turned it on. The second he finished speaking with the team doctor, the phone rang. Seth answered, then talked for a minute, mostly replying with one-word answers before hanging up and putting the H2 in gear.

"That was Mr. Langan," Seth said. "They got word from the league about the steroid thing."

CHAPTER SIXTY-FIVE

SETH GRINNED AT THEM as he pulled slowly out of the parking lot through the crowd. He held out a hand for Troy to slap him five.

Troy slapped his hand into Seth's in slow motion, a questioning look on his face.

"Your DVD recording of Gumble did the trick," Seth said. "The newspaper is printing a full retraction and apologizing to me publicly. Peele got fired, and the commissioner cleared me to play tomorrow."

"Yes!" Troy said, leaning forward to pat Seth on the shoulder with his good hand.

The X-ray showed no break in Troy's finger or hand, but Doctor Garrett still let out a low whistle when Seth told him about Troy taking snaps and even throwing a touchdown pass to finish the game despite the injury. The finger hurt Troy even worse now. It had swollen up like a purple sausage. They packed it in ice, and Doctor Garrett gave Troy some pain medication that left him feeling light-headed by the time they pulled into the driveway of Seth's stone mansion.

Rusty Howell's dad, apparently confident that the team would win, had made a banner that he strung up on the deck overlooking Seth's pool and patio, where the players and parents milled about drinking sodas and eating all kinds of chips under the glare of floodlights. After a few minutes, Nathan's dad arrived from the Kroger with bags full of hot dogs, burgers, and buns. Nathan's dad and Seth went to work at the grill, and everyone talked and laughed and recounted every detail of the game.

At eleven o'clock, almost everyone—more than a hundred people—crowded into Seth's TV room to watch the local news on the big screen. Everyone cheered at the highlights, and roared with laughter at Nathan's crazy end zone dance. There were other highlights on other stations, too, and when they couldn't find anymore, Seth began replaying the clips they'd already seen on his digital recorder.

After a time, people began to move back outside, downing more food and drinks. The pine trees whispered overhead, and a chill began to ride the small breeze. Troy found himself standing by the diving board, talking with Nathan and Tate. Like the rest of the team, they hadn't bothered to change out of their football pants after the game and only wore T-shirts on top. The bag of ice hanging from Troy's hand had begun to leak, and when he reminded them about a certain hit he'd made on the Vipers' quarterback on a third-down play, he swung his hand and accidentally spattered Nathan's face with drops of water. Tate and Troy laughed.

"Sheesh," Nathan said, wiping dry his eyes. "Easy, will you? You didn't hit him *that* hard."

"I put a gouge in my helmet," Troy said, straightening his back.

"No way," Nathan said.

"Come on," Troy said, "My helmet's in Seth's H2. I'll show you."

Together they walked through the enormous house, pausing in front of the big back window to look down on the party.

"I can't believe we're actually here," Tate said in a voice that sounded hushed in the cavernous space of Seth's great room with its twenty-foot ceiling. "*The* Seth Halloway is *our* coach."

"I know," Troy said, feeling quiet himself and even a little small. "Everything really worked out, didn't it? Peele getting canned. Me being able to help the Falcons."

"And us being champs," Tate said, grinning brightly.

"Yeah," Troy said, returning her smile and putting an arm around both her and Nathan. "The best thing of all. Football champs, that's us. Wow. I almost can't believe it."

"You gotta believe it when you know I scored the winning touchdown," Nathan said. "Hey, you trying to distract me from seeing that dent in your helmet that you supposedly got?"

They laughed at him and walked the rest of the way through the house, Troy swinging open the front door.

Troy froze.

Before them stood a tall, thick-boned man with a chiseled jaw and shaggy brown hair. He wore a leather blazer with a narrow pin-striped shirt, jeans, and lizard-skin cowboy boots that gleamed up at them. His dark brown eyes bore into Troy.

"Not another lawyer," Tate said, rolling her eyes.

Troy had told them about the agents and lawyers who approached him after the game, leaving out the amount of money Nash had mentioned.

"Yes," the man said, nodding, "I am a lawyer. Troy, I saw you and your mother on *Larry King*."

"How'd you get past the gates?" Nathan asked.

The man cast a quick look at Nathan, serious and intense enough to make Nathan look down at his feet.

"I'm from out of town, but I have a client who lives in the neighborhood," the man said in a voice softer than his face, "but I came to see you, Troy."

"Because you want to represent me?" Troy asked.

"No," said the man, "because I think I'm your father."